Dedication:

To my good friend, Candacy, for if you never dared me to write a book, I wouldn't have even tried. Thank you for your endless help and encouragement.

To my wonderful mother, Susan Lavender, for you encouraged and guided the idea of writing a book and made me believe I could. Your faith in me was unwavering.

To my husband, Chris, thank you for dealing with my frustrations and endless conversations about writing this book. You helped me like no other. My heart belongs to you.

I love you all.

PROLOGUE

On a typical Friday evening in the Solars' house, it was always 'Ghost Watchers' blaring on the television. Samuel and Abby Solars sat on the couch in their two bedroom conservative home watching the show, as their daughter wandered in and out of the room. She had caught glimpses of the show often dreaming in her head about how one day she was going to grow up and help supernatural beings and ghosts pass to the heavenly side. Abby often wondered if she shouldn't allow little Bekah to watch the show, considering that she was only seven. However, Abby quickly turned her attention back to the television, thinking how she only ran in and out, so she really couldn't be catching that much.

Samuel enjoyed the show as it helped keep his mind off his unsatisfying job as the school janitor. They were always trying to earn enough money to keep their family afloat. Abby, however, watched the show because, as a stay-home mom, she needed some kind excitement and fantasy in her life.

As Bekah was in her room playing with some tattered dolls and worn out blocks, she started feeling unusually tired. She lay down on the unpolished, hardwood floor and dozed into unconsciousness. She awakened a while later, and looked around, wondering why she was on the cold floor. Bekah slowly stood up. With an aching head, she meandered through the hallway, into the living room, and came to a complete stop, as the unfolding scene wasn't what she was expecting or familiar with.

The small, square shaped living room with white painted walls and unfinished, scratched hardwood floors was transformed into a nightmare. She immediately said with a hint of curiosity and confusion in her words, "Mom...Dad?"

As she stared at them, she cautiously walked towards the couch, grasped her father's arm, and shook it gently. She, then, reached for her mother's leg and tapped on it with her now slightly trembling hand. She watched her parents sitting on the couch; they slowly fell, leaning on their sides, and came to a stop on the cushions of the couch.

Bekah's mind started spiraling into confusion. Her breath was getting more short and ragged; her heart felt like it was pounding out of her chest. "Mom!" she now yelled, with an element of fear growing through her voice.

Bekah did a quick scan of the living room. She saw the end credits to the show playing on their television, her father's half-burned cigarette sitting in the ashtray, and the phone receiver was lying on the floor. As her eyes led back to her parents, she took a particular look at the dark red blood trickling down both their foreheads. She noticed both of their eyes were still open, and started getting angry that they wouldn't respond to her like they normally do. She yelled again, "DAD...MOM, what's the matter?!" She felt the burn of tears welling up in her abnormally bright, emerald green eyes, when there was a stern knock at the front door. Bekah's fear took hold of her, and she sprinted to her room.

A multitude of people started to arrive at the Solars' house: police officers, detectives, paramedics and the on-call death examiner. To Bekah, these were just strangers trampling in and out of her house, occasionally calling out her name. However, Bekah remained paralyzed with fear and unable to walk, as she was still trying to process and understand what had just happened. She stayed inside her closet snuggled up with her multiple stuffed animals and tried to stay as quiet as she could through her sniffles and occasional moaning cries. Periodically, the closet door would open and a person would scan the inside, presumably looking for her. After three people attempted to find her, a young man opened the door, looking inside for much longer than any of the other strangers had. Although Bekah sat as still as she could holding her breath, the man locked eyes with her, and carefully pulled Bekah out of the closet.

Bekah was being questioned over and over, but she couldn't find herself able to speak at all. Her throat felt so closed up that she wasn't even sure how air was getting into her lungs, much less how to get any words out. She sat on the wooden kitchen chair, her light brown hair tangled, and strands plastered to her cheeks by the tears she had cried. Keeping her head down, staring at the cold linoleum floor, a pair of dirty brown boots filled her vision. The man who pulled her out of the closet crouched down to her eye level and softly questioned, "I'm sorry, Bekah, to have to ask you this, but you do understand your parents are dead, right, Bekah?" Even though she had that tiny thought in the back of her mind, she hadn't fully processed it all until the man brought the life-changing fact to her full attention. Bekah still wouldn't answer him; new tears formed and streamed down as the realization came that she had just lost the only two people in this world whom loved her unconditionally, and cared for her whole-heartedly.

As the mess of strangers walked out of her house, slowly leaving in their police cars and going about their business, the man who pulled Bekah out of the closet said softly and slowly, "We are going to take a short ride down to the police station, just you and me, and you have no reason to be scared." She looked at him with a bit of speculation across her face, as she didn't trust anyone just yet. They slowly walked out to the dark blue police car that had the word "Sheriff" stenciled on the side. Bekah climbed in the cold, leather back seat. The man fastened her seat belt, and she watched carefully as he walked around the front of the car, and then entered the driver's seat. She heard muffled voices coming over the radio in the police car. Every now and then she heard her parents name or hers. Not really paying attention to them Bekah sat silently, and watched the world go by from the window.

After a short drive, they arrived at the station, and entered a very busy area. A few people were being lead around in handcuffs. One man was yelling loudly in anger, which made Bekah flinch and others just sat next to busy cluttered desks. "It's okay, Bekah. You're safe here," said the Sheriff. He then led Bekah to an empty room, gave her a can of soda, and after lightly patting her on her shoulder, he asked, "I need you to wait here so I can find someone for you. Are you okay with that?" Bekah stared at the man, too scared to speak quite yet and with hesitation on his face, the man left, closing the door behind him.

Bekah sat in the empty room for what seemed like hours, lightly chewing on her shoulder-length hair, and still trying to understand the events of the night. Just then, a dark-brown haired man with wire rimmed glasses entered the room. Bekah immediately jumped off the hard cold steel chair she was sitting on, and slowly stepped backwards until she reached the room's brick wall. He was dressed in blue jeans and a plain green t-shirt. He slowly approached Bekah and said, "Bekah, I am your Uncle Cooper, and I am going to take you home with me. Are you alright with that?" Bekah still had the lump in her throat that wasn't allowing her to talk, but after noticing the bright, emerald green eyes of the soft spoken man, something in her brain registered that allowed her to at least trust the man, even if it was just a little bit.

Bekah started thinking why she hadn't ever met this so-called Uncle before, and she wondered how he knew her. Just as if Bekah had asked those questions out loud, he stated, "I am your father's brother, and at any time if something was to happen to him, it is I who was to look after you." He smiled at her, a warm small smile that showed he cared for her, but at the same time was filled with sorry and pity. So, Bekah inched herself away from the wall, took his hand, and walked out the door.

They drove south of town for approximately fifteen minutes, turned on some gravel roads, and eventually came to a dark blue, A-framed house. To Bekah, it seemed like they were in the middle of nowhere. There were no neighbor's visible, only large trees in the huge yard and the sound of a dog barking from inside the house. It was still dark outside. The only light came from the electric pole that was located just to the right of his house. They entered through the creaky wooden front door. After he grabbed the cute, tri-colored beagle so he couldn't jump on Bekah, Uncle Cooper stated, "This is Mr. Noodles. He won't hurt you." Bekah cautiously reached her hand up to pet the dog. She looked at Cooper and formed a very small but yet noticeable smile.

Cooper led her to a large room with a beautiful wooden twin bed, a matching chest of drawers, and a desk that sat across from it. Bekah noticed her pajamas sitting on the bed, and all of her clothes placed in the corner of the room inside a luggage bag. She quietly walked over to the bed without even thinking of putting on the pajamas. She lay down, and allowed her exhausted small-framed body to fall into a deep uninterrupted slumber.

CHAPTER 1

"That's what I remember the most about my childhood. Horrible isn't it... seeing your parents dead on a couch, and then leaving to live with someone I didn't know." I spoke of the memory like it was nothing but a simple, nondramatic event.

"When did you finally start talking?" asked Gabe.

"The next morning when I woke up starving, and wanting food." Gabe just chuckled softly. I could tell he really didn't know what to say or how to react to the story. "Why the sudden interest in my childhood? Hell, it was thirteen years ago."

Gabe said, looking a little embarrassed for asking, "I was just curious how you got into this line of work, that's all. It's not every day you come across a fellow Ghost Reader. There's not many of us in the world, and after working together for a year now, you'd think that I'd know more." He was right. Very few Ghost Readers existed, but the few of us that did had a unique power to shuffle out the lingering spirits that roamed the world and help them find peace within themselves. We didn't just simply see and talk to ghosts, our powers was very rare and well known to the people of Jasper, Iowa.

Now, I'm not trying to change the subject or anything, but Gabe was definitely my type of man. He was twenty-one years old with beautiful chestnut brown hair that came just above his shoulders. Even if he did comb it, his hair naturally fell into place, the multiple layers surrounding his dimpled cheeks and beautiful, sparkling ocean blue eyes. He was about 6'0" with a toned, athletic body that screamed sexy. I often think we would make a pretty good couple, if that mouth of his didn't constantly talk and ask questions.

I was never one for going out on dates too often. I kept myself busy with my ghosts and cases. They were easier to deal with than living humans. I quickly scanned my 5'6" body up and down noticing what used to be light-brown hair had changed over the years and was now more of a dark-brown color that had reached my middle back. My size six, not-too-slender, but toned, one hundred thirty pound body and my natural lightly tanned skin made me think we wouldn't look too bad together. That thought, however, like most thoughts about Gabe didn't linger too long in my head.

It was getting late in the afternoon and about closing time at the shop when Gabe asked, "Do you want to go get a bite to eat?" He was shoving papers in his bag and gathering his things to leave.

"Um, can we go to Del's Diner?" I already knew the answer to that question before he gave it.

"You spend most of your time and day in that damn diner, Bekah. Can't you go somewhere else and just forget about things for a while?" Gabe shook his head in frustration.

I answered with a quick and sharp, "No," and noticed Gabe was already walking out the front door stating, "Night, I will see you in the morning." He asked me quite often if I'd go to dinner with him and our conversation always ended the same way. I quickly put away my files and cleaned up my usual cluttered desk. After locking the door, I walked down to the corner of McKins Street, where Del's was located.

Now you have to understand that Del's isn't just an ordinary town diner where local people went to have their morning coffee and catch up on the latest town gossip. Del's was special; the air around it was just a tad bit chillier, so whenever you walked by goose bumps crawled over your skin and, on occasion, there was a spark of static electricity in the air. This would make sense after you realized that Del's wasn't just filled with lively town's people, but also with ghosts...lots of ghosts. Apparitions from all over the world were drawn to this one place. The majority of people couldn't see, hear, or even acknowledge that a ghost was in their presence, but I was very different in that aspect.

As I walked into the diner I saw Joe. He was sitting in his usual spot, the corner booth of the diner, and reading a newspaper. I have no idea why he read the newspaper, because, as a ghost, he really couldn't do anything. I always just assumed that Joe, being from this little town of Jasper wanted to keep up with the local news. He was a middle-aged man, mid-fifties; he had led a happy life with his wife and three children. However, he suffered a massive heart attack and died. He had a yellowish aura around him, which told me he was content with his previous life, with no regrets or unfinished business he needed to resolve. "Hi, Joe!" I said enthusiastically as I passed by him. I liked chatting with him. He usually knew all the town gossip and filled me in on a daily basis.

"Hey, Bekah, grab a seat with me!" Joe called back. I strolled over to the booth and sat across from him.

"So you heard about the Meads, right? The younger son was found today drowned in the lake... tragic. I heard the cops talking about it when they were in earlier," Joe said shaking his head.

Looking a bit surprised I responded, "No, but maybe I will see him soon...or you will." Joe also had a good knack at keeping his eyes open for any new ghosts that arrived to the diner.

"It's none of your damned business, if you ask me." I heard a raspy, grumpy old voice over my shoulder. I knew exactly who that was the moment he spoke a word: Walter.

"Thank you for your input, Walter," I said a bit sarcastically, but with a smile as he walked by.

Walter was an older man, I guessed in his eighties, with fine white hair on the sides of his head; he was grumpy, not merely a little grouchy because he was feeling the aches of his arthritis or didn't sleep well. He was naturally a cantankerous, cranky old man who didn't mind speaking exactly what entered his mind. He did, however, have a yellow aura around him, which told me that Walter wasn't angry or displeased, but rather a content and happy man whom had a naturally disgruntled nature.

Ghosts with the yellowish aura didn't prove to be a problem. They simply chose to stick in limbo, rather than moving on to the next phase of their journey. Joe, as he had mentioned to me before, stuck around because his wife came in often to the diner, and it gave him a chance to see her and ensure she was doing well. His wife was well aware that he hung around the diner. She would purposely leave a note under her plate just for him. She would update him on their children and other life events. I could tell she really missed Joe, just as he really missed her. He always got a rather somber face when she would leave the diner.

Walter? I still hadn't figured out why he hung around, but as long as he was happy with himself, then I was fine with him, too. I never had the guts to ask Walter too many personal questions. Actually, I don't ask him any questions, but that doesn't stop him from voicing his opinions.

Del's was a rectangular-shaped diner with tables, booths, and bar stools at the counter where customers could chit-chat with the waitresses. The diner had a homey feeling to it, decorated with off white tables and dark blue booths and chairs. All of the walls were of dark wood paneling wainscoted with brick on top. There was matching diamond-shaped, dark blue and off-white ceramic tiling on the floor. There were a few pictures scattered throughout the walls for decoration, but one wall in particular behind the bar was covered with newspaper articles of different people who grew up in Jasper, Iowa. Some included the local high school basketball team's accomplishments or past residents that made it big in the city. I particularly liked the article of Joe. He was quite handsome back in his day, with his dark hair smoothed back, broad shoulders, and dimpled chin. It showed him holding a huge one-hundred and fifty pound catfish from the local lake. He was smiling and quite proud of himself.

I ordered a simple cheeseburger with tater tots from Deon. She was the oldest waitress in Del's and had worked there for her whole life. Deon was nice, out-going, and rather loud as she yelled her orders to the back kitchen, and she apparently liked her make-up because I never saw her without an entire mask on. It was easy to tell Deon had been waitressing for a long time with the way she would carry multiple plates on her arms without a bit of worry to dropping them. No other new ghosts seemed to be visiting this evening, which was a shame because I had a list of people I kept my eye out for to help bring closure to families.

That's how I make my living. You see, people come to me as they find out that I'm a Ghost Reader and ask for my services in finding out what happened to their loved ones. Gabe was my partner. He was also a Ghost Reader and we worked together to do one of three things: help a ghost pass over into its heaven, if it so desired to, help a ghost make its way in this life living in limbo peacefully, if it wanted, or, to tame the really angry ghosts to a point that they were manageable and didn't cause trouble to others, living or not. It was the third option, from what Uncle Cooper told me, that was the most exhausting, and time consuming task to accomplish.

CHAPTER 2

As I waited patiently for my food to arrive and curve my hungry stomach, I thought about the first time I ever met a ghost. It was the middle of January on a cold winter day. I arrived home from school and my Uncle Cooper wished me a happy thirteenth birthday. He took me to eat at Del's. As we were waiting to have our order taken, I saw a glimpse of a whitish-gray figure sitting on the floor behind the bar stools. I remember how odd it was that the figure had a soft blue glow around it and asked my Uncle who it was. He said with a matter-of-fact expression, "Well, that's a ghost, and a sad one at that." The little ghost girl was younger than I was at that time, I guessed about eleven years old. She was weeping, looking confused and scared. I wandered over to the bar stools and stared at the girl with a curious look on my face.

The girl then said through her sobs, "Please help me find my Daddy." I took a step back, thinking that maybe I was going crazy. I, then, quickly rushed back to my table as my food was waiting for me and it seemed like a good enough reason to get away from the now talking ghost.

I ate slowly, still eyeing the girl as she huddled against the wall with her knees drawn up to her chest. She continued sobbing and, on occasion, would glance up at me. Finally, my Uncle said, "So are you going to talk to her, or just watch her cry?" He smiled at me, "It's ok, and she won't hurt you. She just needs your help."

With caution and hesitation I walked back over to the little girl and asked her, "What's your name?"

The small, frail girl looked up, and quietly stated, "Emily."

I introduced myself and sat across from her on the floor. I asked softly, "Why are you here?"

Emily took a deep breath in and started to explain, "I was in my Dad's car on the way home from a friend's house. He was driving, and we were both singing to the radio when, in an instant, I felt his arm slam across my chest. I wasn't sure what was happening, and then, as everything started to go black in my eyes, I looked over to where my Dad should've been, and he wasn't there." I took this in as Emily spoke, feeling bad for her as she talked about not being able to find her father.

"What did you do next?" I asked, wanting to learn more.

Emily responded, "I'm not sure. I know I fell asleep, but when I woke up I could see my body still in the car. But my father was still gone. I started walking around the car to try and find him, but I never did. Then, I felt something kind of tugging at me, like a gnawing feeling telling me where to go, and I ended up here, in this diner."

"What's your Dad's name?" I asked her.

With tears refilling her eyes she replied, "Henry."

"Well, I'm not sure what exactly I can do to help you, but if I can I will," I continued, "I'm very sorry you are so sad." I didn't know what else I could do, so I walked away back to my Uncle as I continued to hear Emily sob.

My Uncle continued eating his food, and he watched me return. He said with a calm, soothing voice, "She is sad."

"How did you know?" I naively asked.

"Other than the tears," he chuckled, "I can tell by her glowing aura. You see, Bekah, the blue glow means that deep down inside her she's very sad. Ghosts have different auras, and after you learn these you will know exactly how that ghost is feeling." I took a moment to consider this and make a mental note. My Uncle then said, "Why don't you go hug her, so maybe she won't feel so alone?" He gave me an encouraging smile and nodded his head towards her as I made my way back to Emily. She looked up through her shoulder length blond hair and came toward me. I really wasn't quite sure how to hug a ghost, but I put my arms out to reach around her. The moment I touched her shoulder, my mind went spiraling out of control.

It felt like I was on a roller coaster, unable to make sense of where I was or catch up with myself. Suddenly, my mind came to a halt and I found myself in a car, singing "Baby Baby" with a man in the driver's seat. The words ran out of my mouth fluently as if I had heard the song a million times. I was smiling and giggling while watching the man sing along and make funny faces at me. The world around me seemed to be in slow motion. Looking out the window, I could take in every detail of my surroundings.

I was just outside Rhoades, a small town about thirty miles from Jasper, traveling on a two lane highway as the speedometer read sixty-five mph. The heated air was blowing from the vents to keep them warm. However, the very first thing I noticed was how freely she could move. She had no seat belt across her, which allowed her to wiggle and dance as she sat in the front seat.

The man driving was heavyset with blond, shaggy hair and an untrimmed mustache. This was Henry, as I could feel the love and adoration coming from Emily's mind. Out of the corner of my eye, I saw the shiny patch of black ice in the middle of the road. I couldn't warn Henry, even though I tried by yelling at him. He quickly threw his arm around me and the car slammed trying to stop, making high pitched noises as the brakes tried to accommodate to the declining speed. With a look of horror upon the blond man's face, the car screeched sideways in the road and finally came to a full stop after flying off the side of the highway into a deep embankment.

The front of the car was smashed in, pushing the motor and metal of the car backwards. I watched Henry get forced out of the front seat, break through the window shield, and come to a body-jolting thud onto the snow-covered grass, after he smacked into the trunk of large tree. My body slung into the dash board of the car. I could feel my ribs cracking apart one at a time. A sudden and sever pain shot through my chest as I tried to breathe in. My organs shoved against my hard bones, and my head pounded into the solid glass of the side window. I looked over to find Henry, scared and confused. I felt my eyes get heavy, and blacked out in the front seat of the car. I knew right then Emily was dead, as I could no longer feel the intense beating of her heart.

My mind quickly pulled back to my own and I immediately started shaking and trembling, feeling exhausted all over as I tried to make sense of what just happened. I felt like I was going to puke. I felt a hand on my shoulder as Uncle Cooper said, "Just relax, Bekah. Let yourself get reacquainted with where you are." I took deep breaths to help slow my breathing and decrease the shaking in my limbs. I stared up at my Uncle in disbelieve and awaiting an explanation of what had just happened, but instead he gently smiled and calmly spoke the words, "You are a Ghost Reader, Bekah."

CHAPTER 3

The smell of cheeseburgers and tots brought me back to my senses and I quickly started to eat. Joe was gone now, and I was sitting alone at the booth. Del's had the best cheeseburgers in the area and was well known in the town of Jasper. Of course, Jasper was a relatively small town with a population of about 5000 people. Nestled about an hour drive from the big city of Des Moines, Iowa, the town wasn't really known for much of anything other than a place where ghosts gather.

Delbert, the owner of Del's Diner, was use to the occasional person entering and talking to an unseen person. He had been good friends with my Uncle Cooper and allowed him to do his work without intervening or questioning. There, of course, had been no surprise to him when he started seeing me speak to invisible people. Del would go on about his day, running his diner and cooking the food. He had no intentions of trying to stop any situations unless someone was getting hurt.

I finished up my dinner, paid at the register, and then began my walk back to the office where I had left my car. After a couple blocks I jumped in my black Ford Explorer and started the drive home. It was the same drive I took from the police station so many years ago; it took me about fifteen minutes to drive to the A-framed house my Uncle had lived in.

It remained dark blue in color with multiple trees in the yard. I still had no neighbors close to me, and being out in the country meant it was nice and quiet, perfect place for a person like me to relax and recharge my mind. I entered the house, wishing to see Uncle Cooper, but knowing all too well he was no longer there. I missed chatting with him about the different ghosts I would encounter, but Cooper had decided after his death that he would move on to his heaven. He always said he didn't want to hang around Jasper forever, so he said a quick good-bye to me and disappeared. He knew he had taught me everything I needed to know. I hadn't seen him since, not at Del's, nor anywhere else.

Uncle Cooper was a funny, outgoing, smart, and very clean man. He had lived in this place alone, never married, and didn't have any children of his own. He wasn't very tall for a man, standing at 5'8". He had very short dark brown hair, kept almost like a crew cut, and, of course, the same bright, emerald green colored eyes I had. I hadn't ever asked him why he never married, but I always assumed that the ghost reading thing played into his reasoning. Uncle Cooper was always one to be open when asked questions, but rarely did he give any information on his own. He liked his privacy, peace and quiet.

I jumped into the shower and enjoyed the nice hot water before drying off. I slipped in to a two-size bigger t-shirt and climbed into the soft pillow top queen bed. It wasn't very late, but I flicked on my television to help turn off my mind. I had a bad habit of allowing thoughts to keep me awake, so I used the television to help relief them and allowed myself to succumb to sleep.

My dreams took me back to a time when I was learning about being a Ghost Reader with my Uncle Cooper. He was very knowledgeable about ghosts, and taught me everything I could store in my brain. Uncle Cooper instructed me about the different auras that surround ghosts and how to approach each one. He gave me advice on how to control the after effects of leaving a ghost's mind. But the very last thing he taught me was how evil certain ghosts are that have a dark, purplish-black aura. These ghosts were filled with such rage and anger they couldn't be helped or guided to finding their peaceful state. They needed to be sent straight to Hell for their evil wrong doings, which wasn't something we were capable of doing. These ghosts were dangerous and able to hurt living human beings.

Those were the apparitions that I feared the most, because prior to my Uncle's passing, I hadn't ever dealt with these ghosts firsthand. My Uncle had briefly stated he came across one many years ago, but he wasn't able to control him. The only sure thing he could tell me was the after effects of leaving those particular ghosts' minds were far worse than a yellow, blue, or red aura ghosts.

I awoke that September morning smiling, knowing that Uncle Cooper had probably visited me in my dreams somehow to remind me of my ghostly inclinations and skills. I did, however, have a small bit of fear in the very back of my head, causing me to wonder if I would ever have to come up against a purple-black aura, dangerous, evil ghost.

CHAPTER 4

I arrived at the office about nine a.m. that next Friday morning and found Gabe sitting behind his desk with a rather intense frown on his face. "Don't you ever look at your cell phone?" he asked irritated.

"Yes, but when I know it's you, I just ignore it," I replied rather tartly; and no, I hadn't even glanced at it. Gabe knew how to push my buttons at times, and the last thing I wanted to do was start my morning off squabbling with him.

"Whatever," he softly replied.

I often glanced at Gabe as he sat behind his desk or walked around the office. I would notice his lazy shuffle on the non-busy days and how he would smile when he was thinking about something that made him happy. The way he would curl his lips up just right to form those ever-so-cute dimples in his cheeks or laugh out loud, forming a full grin complimenting his all-around sexiness. His strong arms would flex, and I took explicit notice when he wore a cut off t-shirt that showed his perfectly formed biceps. Then, on occasion, as he shifted his bright, ocean-blue eyes at me when I least expected it, I would look down quickly, and rather sheepishly, hoping inside he didn't notice. "So the reason I called you about fifteen times was because we got a new one at Del's...and he's an angry one."

"A red aura?" I asked, although I pretty much already knew the answer.

"Yep, male, looks to be in his thirties and keeping quiet for the moment, but the redness is just rolling off him," Gabe explained.

"How did you find out about this one?" I asked.

"Well," he stated with a bit of smirk to his voice, "if you look at your desk you will figure it out." I ambled over to my desk without any great hurry and found a Del's Diner styrofoam cup full of cappuccino with my favorite type of danish right next to it.

I smiled and asked, "Is it pumpkin spice? 'Cause you know that's my favorite."

Gabe replied with a small smirk on his face, "Of course it is, and the danish is strawberry...just how you like." I couldn't help but smile at him, feeling kind of special inside that he remembered what my usual breakfast was, and how really thankful I was that he got it, because I didn't stop prior to arriving at the office.

"Thanks, Gabe," I said as the smile stayed across my face.

"Anytime, if it means seeing that smile," Gabe stated with a grin.

"Aww, aren't you sweet this morning?" I flirtatiously asked. Every now and then I would let my guard down. I knew Gabe had some feelings for me. I wasn't exactly sure what those feelings were, but he did occasionally do something that made me wonder.

"I'd be even sweeter if you would let me take you out to dinner...somewhere other than your usual," he taunted with a sexy grin. "What's wrong with going out on one date, Bekah? Am I not your type?" he stated as he sat in his desk chair.

I quickly cleared my throat, took a swallow of my cappuccino, and asked, "So, how do you want to do this?"

Gabe formed those dimples again, raised his eyebrows and replied, "Well, I don't mind taking it one step at a time if you don't. I know you have trust issues." He spun around in his desk chair like a little kid sitting on it their first time.

A bit of surprise ran through my face as I stated, "I meant the angry ghost, Gabe. How are we going to handle this? Are you doing the reading or me?"

"Oh, that" he said, not really minding that he misunderstood the question, "I think I better take it. He could be a bit stronger than usual, and all that anger tends to make them unpredictable; easier for them to build walls in their heads, and not allowing us to read him well. That and I'm a guy, so he may feel more inclined not to fight than if a woman tried reading him." Gabe looked up at me with a serious face as if he made some remarkable statement.

"Okay, I can see that, but being a woman doesn't make me less powerful, you realize that, right?" I responded, making sure I kept my pride intact.

"Oh, of course, Bekah, I wouldn't ever imply anything that ridiculous. You're very strong in your reading abilities," he said as he smiled that cute grin that made me go red in the cheeks.

"Well, let's get going then." I quickly ate my danish and swallowed the last of the cappuccino.

Gabe swung the door, held it open for me and in his best British accent he stated, "Your door, my Lady," which made me giggle as I tried not to choke on my last bite.

Immediately after entering Del's Diner, I spotted the angry ghost. He was tall, about 6'3", long, curly red hair, looked to be about in his thirties as Gabe had mentioned, and definitely was spewing some red aura about him. His eyes flashed red at times and his lips were pursed closed.

I remembered back to my training with Uncle Cooper when he told me about the red aura ghosts. They aren't as easy to confront. They are angry, maybe because they are dead, possibly because they were killed in an angry way, or maybe simply because they are confused and don't understand what is happening to them. The best way to confront these types is head-on, strong-willed and matter-of-factly.

"I go this," Gabe stated as he took in a deep breath and walked right up to the ghost. Gabe wasn't quite eye level with him as he had about three inches on him, but quickly and straight-to-the-point he said, "I'm going to touch your shoulder and when I do, I will enter your mind. I will then be able to read you, see exactly why you are so angry, and figure out what we can do to help you. Do you understand me?" The tall ghost looked down at him. A quick flash of blood red briefly filled his brown eyes. He raised both arms up in the air and threw them down on Gabe's shoulders. Of course, this didn't hurt Gabe, but he flinched, just briefly, as he thought of how it would feel. He closed his mind, as to not enter the ghosts mind at that moment.

The ghost very angrily stated, "Oh, hell no, you're not. No one is probing around my mind. Just try it you little prick and see where it gets you!!!"

Gabe stared back at him and without releasing his gaze reached out his hand and stated, "Well, this could be interesting." As his hand drew closer to his shoulder, the ghost caught Gabe's arm mid-air, and after seeing his sly grin, he then quickly realized that he just gave Gabe his way in.

That much familiar voice came from behind me as I heard Walter say, "I like him, he called Gabe a prick!! Ha!" I patiently waited in the diner, and continued to sip on my cappuccino as Gabe was reading the ghosts mind.

Reading can usually take a few minutes to an hour; depending on how long the ghost tries to fight you off or how many memories you were processing. The longer we stayed inside a ghosts mind, the harsher the after effects were. However, most angry ghosts were confused, and that could make it easier to get past the walls they put in their brain, not always though. I knew the minute Gabe was in, as his body relaxed, shoulders fell forward, and his head bobbed down. Rarely did we ever fall over when we entered a mind, as our body naturally stood on its own two feet, relaxed and at ease. However, whenever there was a struggle to get complete access to the ghost's mind, our bodies were often very tense with muscle spasms or mild jerking all over, and we were then known to fall over.

As I was drinking a soda and waiting for Gabe to release the ghosts mind, Joe popped up behind me and said "Gotta mad one there, huh? I tried talking to him, but he wouldn't have anything to do with me. He just kept saying, 'How could she?' I do believe whatever is troubling the man has to do with a woman."

"Well, damn. Isn't that typical?" smarted off Walter. I thanked Joe for his information, and began scanning the diner.

The breakfast crowd was winding down and Delbert was behind the cook's window prepping food for the lunch rush. Delbert smiled and waved for me to come over. As I approached him, he stated, "You know, I still got that waitressing job open if you're ever interested in changing your job path."

I just smiled at him and said, "But, Delbert, it wouldn't be nearly as interesting and exhausting as the job I currently have." He and I both chuckled.

"True, but in all seriousness, I saw what a toll it took on Cooper at times. I hate to see you go down the same stressful path." He continued, "Just know you always have a job here if you change your mind." He kissed me softly on my forehead as I thanked him for his concern and resumed my previous task of watching over Gabe.

Occasionally, I would glance at Delbert as he was cutting up potatoes or preparing hamburgers. He was an older man in his early sixties, standing about 5'9" with a medium build; his black hair showing gray steaks of age through it. I thought of Delbert like a father-figure now that Uncle Cooper was gone. He did his best to make sure I got food in my belly and plenty of rest. He had nothing but the best intentions for me. If I were ever to enter a ghost's mind by myself in the diner, he always made it a point to keep an eye on me. Of course, then he would lecture me for doing it by myself and not having Gabe there for back up.

Approximately twenty-five minutes passed before I saw Gabe straighten up his body and lower himself to the floor. I rushed to his side, reminding him that he was okay and to take deep breaths. Gabe looked at me with a tired face and said, "I'm okay, Bekah. I got this one figured out."

"Well, tell me what happened, Gabe. How did he die, and why is he so mad? As much detail as you can, please." Looking over at the ghost I noticed him walking away, past a row of tables, and into the kitchen. His aura seemed a little less red, and it wasn't seeping around him as much as before. Gabe had caught his breath and, trying to ease the tremors, he started to explain what he saw.

"His name is Hank. He was married, had three kids, and considered himself a hard-working, loyal husband who generally put in sixty or more hours a week at his job. He drove to his construction worksite as he routinely did almost every morning." Gabe described the event as he remembered with clear detail, and not having any difficulty reading the ghost's mind. "He was thinking that morning how he really didn't want to go to work and maybe a short day was in order. He had finished laying the plans to the office building structure he was designing, gave his orders to his crew and headed to his big, red Ford F-250 to leave for home early. He thought how the kids were in school and his wife was probably just cleaning around the house or running a few errands, so he would surprise her by showing up and helping her out. He stepped out of his truck and immediately noticed a dark blue Dodge Charger sitting along the side of the road in front of his house. He entered his home, walked through the dark green painted front living room and headed down the hall to his bedroom, all the while calling out his wife's name, Cheryl. As he turned to open his bedroom door, he thought how odd it was that it was even closed, as they always kept the door open. You see where this is going, don't ya, Bekah?" Gabe asked while rubbing his forehead with his still trembling fingers.

"Yes, I'm getting a pretty good idea, but continue anyways." I insisted.

Gabe continued his story, "He walked into the fairly large bedroom, painted dark brown with blue trim around the two windows, and saw his wife lying on top of a much younger man. The man had dirty blond hair, and not necessarily a great body...not that I really pay a lot of attention to that. He had slight muscle tone that gave some definition to his muscles, but otherwise pretty average. Hank was trying to remember if he had ever seen this man before, and if so, where from? Before he could even finish that thought, he got angry, very angry, at the sight of what he just walked into, in the bedroom of his own house," Gabe sucked in a deep breath of air and rambled on, "You have to understand that this was a house that he designed, built specifically for him and his wife to raise their children and retire in someday." Gabe briefly paused and relaxed his body in continued efforts to calm the trembling muscles and making sure he had his thoughts all gathered correctly so he could describe the events accurately.

I replied, "So she's a lying, cheating wife. I understand why he is so angry now. Go on." Gabe slightly raised his eyebrows and nodded his head yes. He continued describing the events.

"As he stood there in the doorway, he was trying to decide just how he was going to handle this situation. But the more he thought and watched with his eyes, the feelings of betrayal, and anger sent his blood boiling with fury. He immediately grabbed his wife and threw her onto the cream-colored carpeted floor. She lied there naked, tears flowing out her eyes, apologizing for what a huge mistake she had been making. He then went after the unfamiliar man. He had already been making his way off the bed when Hank had pulled his arm back and punched him straight in the nose. The stunned man, now with bright red blood streaking down his lips and chin, did not take this well. He immediately went charging after Hank yelling, "What the hell, man? You broke my nose!!!"

"Hank replied, 'Well, that's not all I'm going to break, you ugly-ass son of a bitch!!' Hank grabbed the man by his shoulders, kneed him in the gut, and tossed him to the floor opposite of his crying wife. The man lies there, catching his breath and looked to be thinking how he had to get out of there before he got killed. His face had smeared blood all over and even more bright red blood streaming down his face, dripping from his chin. Hank paused for a minute, in disbelief of what his wife did. Such betrayal he never knew she was capable of. The beaten man slowly stood up and started making his way out of the bedroom, stumbling through the hallway to the very large front living room." Gabe paused for a moment. "Hank made an extra effort to meet him there and again, grabbed the man, throwing him head first into the brick lined fire place. The younger man grabbed his head, shook it ever so slightly, and blinked his eyes a few times as if trying to see past the stars that were circling around him. He saw Hank approaching him again and became desperate to do anything to stop him. He grabbed the fireplace log poker and swung as hard as he could. He waited, with his eyes closed for the worst to happen, but soon realized Hank had fallen over onto the floor. I knew Hank had died immediately, right then and there with that slam of the poker against his right temple. Ah, hell, Bekah. This is crazy." Gabe slowed a bit. I grabbed him a soda from Del to help clear his throat and alleviate his dry mouth.

"So he died pissed off and is still pissed off. What exactly does he want, Gabe? Revenge?" I asked as I was attempting to have complete understanding of the situation.

"Aww, did that take you a while to come up with, Bekah?" again smarted Walter.

"Not now, Walter. Cut me a little slack, ok?" I sassed back.

"No, not revenge exactly," said Gabe with a bit of a puzzling look on his face. "More like an understanding of why his wife would commit such a horrible act. He's quite pleased with himself about the beating he gave the other guy. Hank's just really pissed at his wife and wants clarification. However, he wishes her no harm. You have to understand that Hank was completely in love with his wife and every hour he worked he did for her. He wanted her to have a life filled with no worries or wants, financially or otherwise. He thought that was what he was doing. So his wife's betrayal really caught him off guard."

Gabe was more himself now, breaths even, body still, and in complete control of his actions. I asked, "So, shall we hunt down this cheating wife and try to get answers for Hank? Or are we just going to take turns trying to calm him ourselves?" This is what Uncle Cooper meant by trying to manage the angry ghosts, to bring them to a level where they weren't so mad. It can take a while, days, sometimes weeks, to lower their level of anger to a level of sadness, or even better, to a place where they are happy again.

Gabe responded, "Well, if you want to take a long road trip, we could, but considering he was from Colorado, I really don't think you'd want to take that course of action. I nudged his mind towards thinking that he can forgive his wife and shoved in a few waves of happiness. Honestly, even with both of us doing that it will take some time to bring down his anger. I say we wait, give him a few days to blow off steam, and see if he won't calm himself down some. He can't hurt anyone, so..."

I paced in front of the booth where I usually sat, walking the line on the floor that showed where the tiles met, and taking into consideration everything he just said. "Oh yeah, God forbid you stay away from this diner for more than one damn day, Bekah. It might fall apart if you were to leave." Walter was really feeling his oats today.

"Alright, Gabe, we will wait three days. If he doesn't calm down, or seems to start getting worse, then we jump in a car and drive. Hopefully he will find his own resolution and we can go about our daily routine. Agreed?" I turned and looked at Walter, "Is that okay with you, Walter? Is there anything else *you* wish to add?"

Walter just grumbled, "Humph!"

"Whatever you say, boss," Gabe said as he smiled at me. Dammit, he knew I hated it when he called me that, which is probably why he threw it out there every once in a while. Gabe and I were equal partners in this job, and he was well aware of it.

"Fine, since I'm the *boss,* I will check on him every evening over the weekend and you take the mornings," I stated. Gabe looked at me, knowing that he was already regretting his choice of name for me.

He took a deep breath and whined, "What? Wait a minute. Why am I checking on him in the mornings? Why don't I take the evenings, and you scout out the mornings? I know how much you like breakfast so you could do both at once. You know I hate waking up in the mornings."

"Well, let's think about this, shall we? I live fifteen minutes out of town. You live three minutes away from our office. If you really wanted to be a dedicated and loyal co-worker, you would take both. I'm sure you get enough beauty rest, Gabe," I said with a little irritation in my voice.

"Like any amount of beauty sleep will help him! Hasn't yet anyway," Walter grumbled.

"Oh, fine. Since you were so sweet about it, I'll take the mornings. Hopefully he will figure things out, because I don't think I'd like to ride all the way to Colorado with you," Gabe said jokingly.

Walter yelled from the kitchen, "I wouldn't walk across town with her!" I rolled my eyes, casually shook my head and turned towards the door of Del's.

As Gabe headed to the door he yelled, "As for you Walter, I think you need a grouchy nap, maybe it will change your attitude a little."

We both walked down the block to our office, I twirled around and faced Gabe. With a smirk on my face I stated, "I don't know, Gabe. I was thinking maybe a road trip with you would be fun." His eyes momentarily lit up and slowly a smile formed. I giggled inside and thought to myself that I was fairly certain I took him off guard

CHAPTER 5

I woke up Sunday morning about seven a.m., reached my arms up over my head, arched my back and felt the first stretch of the day. It was a cool morning so I opted for a long-sleeved, purple thermal top and pair of relaxed fit blue jeans. Yesterday's visit to Del's didn't prove to be very eventful as Hank seemed to be in the same mind frame as he was on Friday. For that matter, so was Walter. Hank still had the red aura surrounding him, but the bubbling and seething didn't seem to be getting any worse.

I didn't do much most of the day; laundry and simple cleaning around the house. I decided I'd just grab some lunch at Del's since I had to drive in to do my check on Hank. I grabbed my cell phone, keys, and wallet, and then headed out the door towards my Explorer. I drove the roads that I could probably drive in my sleep, as I've traveled them frequently. Momentarily I thought about how I never locked my house doors since very few people even drove out in that direction from town. Rarely did I have any visitors, and the few I did have always made me aware when they were coming. Uncle Cooper's dog, Mr. Noodles, was always really good at letting us know when someone was coming down the driveway. However, he was no longer with me either, so I probably should get in the habit of locking up.

I made the drive and pulled into a parking spot at Del's. The moment I walked in the door, I could see that Hank was different. He was spewing dark, red aura all around him, and his face was locked in a grimace. The moment he saw me, he became even more agitated and his pace quickened as he hovered in the dining area.

"What the hell is going on? I don't understand, and I want to know what is happening!" Hank yelled at me. He paused for a moment and then continued in a low, grumbling voice, "I know you can hear me, and so can he." He nodded his head in the general direction towards the corner of the diner.

I scanned the place and my eyes met up with Gabe, sitting in our usual booth just watching the scene unfold. "And he won't say a damn word!!" Hank added.

I calmly approached Hank, trying my best to not allow him to see I was starting to get a little scared, and said, "I can help you, but I need you to get a hold of yourself a little first." He just huffed and continued pacing the floor. His red aura was definitely flowing rapidly and boiling. I headed over towards Gabe, stared at him with a befuddled and frustrated look on my face. Gabe just shrugged his shoulders and shook his head side to side slowly. When I reached him I said with a bit of a hushed tone, but still rather irritated, "What the hell is going on, Gabe? Why are you even here? I thought I had the evening check, and why haven't you said anything? He is clearly much worse than yesterday, and you're just sitting there?"

Gabe continued just staring at me with a complacent look on his face. I could tell he was just waiting for me to shut up so he could speak, but dammit I was the one now getting pissed. Gabe stared back at me and finally stated, "Well, I know I'm going to sound like a broken record...but if you," his teeth clenched closed, "*looked at your phone every once in a while*, you would know, Bekah!" I grabbed my cell out of my pocket, and saw four missed calls and two text messages.

"Damn," I said softly to myself realizing that I really had to get better at this phone stuff. Gabe was obviously getting irritated that I didn't take his calls. But it's not just his calls I didn't take; hell, I hardly ever looked at my phone, and it didn't help that the settings were on silent. The first text message read:

Afternoon Bekah, I'm goin n2 Del's tonight so I can check on Hank

Well, damn, I could've taken a nap. Second message:

Hank gettn worse, nvmd u better get n here

Then, the four missed calls followed the texts. I looked at Gabe and saw he had quite a smug, satisfactory look at his face. I said, "Ok, ok, I will get better at the phone thing." Dang, even with a smug face he was cute.

I looked back around the diner, and saw that Hank was still pacing. The diner was getting full of customers for the Sunday dinner rush. Everyone was enjoying their food, conversing with their family, and completely unaware that an angry ghost was walking amongst them. I could see a look of fascination upon some of their faces when they would see a chair slightly move by itself or a table scoot an inch or two across the floor. As long as Hank didn't pick up anything and throw it, we would be fine. Thankfully, he couldn't physically touch anyone, but that didn't mean he couldn't pick up a salt shaker and pop someone in the head with it.

I watched Hank as he left the dining area and strutted to the kitchen. I followed him, stopped in front of the grill, and said, "If you will promise to keep your cool for a couple more days, I will drive to Colorado and try to get the answers you are seeking, but you *have* to keep yourself as calm as possible." Hank stopped pacing and looked at me while he considered my request. His shoulders and chest heaved down and his facial muscles relaxed.

"Fine," he said more focused, "I will wait here for your return. I wouldn't mind going with you, but I know if I do then I'd probably lose it again at my house. No telling what stupid thing I'd do. Just find out why she went to another man." He walked away and entered Delbert's office. He returned shortly with a piece of paper that contained his wife's name and address.

I returned to Gabe and said, "Well, get to packing, partner, we are taking that road trip."

Gabe just kind of smiled and said, "Great, I always wanted to see the mountains, and now I get to see them with you." I just ignored that last part and walked back to my Explorer. Guess I was heading home to get a few things.

I woke up early the next morning and started packing. Soon I was holding a suitcase packed with the usual items for a trip: clothes, bathroom stuff, phone charger...the essentials. I grabbed an extra jacket, as I knew Colorado could be a bit colder this time of year. I specifically remembered looking at my phone prior to leaving my house in case I didn't hear it go off, but thankfully there were no texts or calls. I locked the doors at my house since I was going to be gone a few days and stopped by the bank in town to grab some cash. Then, I met up with Gabe at his house.

He lived just north of our office in a perfectly square, pale green, one bedroom house on the corner of Meadows St. It had an adorable white, covered porch on the front with matching white window trim, and was just two blocks from our office on McKins Street. He had it pretty good being so close. "Hey," I said as I entered his door.

Gabe looked up as he was zipping his luggage closed, and said, "So we're taking my car, right?"

I glanced up at him with my eyebrows raised, thinking how I knew that wasn't going to happen, and replied, "Oh, I don't think so, Gabe. I would like to at least stretch my legs out from time to time on the long ride there. That dinky '94 Talon isn't even big enough to hold our luggage." Gabe's car was the usual sporty car that guys liked to drive around. It was older, but he kept it in good shape, replacing parts as needed and keeping it clean. However, there was hardly any room in it, as it was only a two door, and not designed for comfortable long trips.

"I will take turns driving with you in *my* car so we don't get too tired. Sound good?" Gabe thought it over and I knew he wasn't thinking about what car we would take, but more about how he could get something else his way if he agreed to my idea. He quickly said, "Fine, but I get to pick what music we listen to."

He grabbed a few CD's from his collection sitting on top of his stereo. I could already imagine listening to sounds of Disturbed, Stone Sour and Seether with a little Van Halen thrown in there. However, that didn't bother me, because I did like that type of music and I knew deep down that I would control the seek buttons on the radio. Gabe grabbed his luggage and went to load it in the back of my Explorer. He tossed his CD's in the front seat and went back to his house to lock it up. After one last final scan inside and deciding he had all he needed, we both headed out to my car.

Gabe immediately went to the driver's side, opened the door, climbed in, and started adjusting the seats to fit his gorgeous body. "Um, what are you doing? I was going to drive first."

He lifted his head to look at me and said, "Well, I'm already here and comfy so you can take second shift." He smiled and winked at me with that boyish grin across his face. I hated when he did that, because it showed those damn cute dimples, and there was just no way that I could argue with him. I walked around the front of the car and slipped into the passenger side, intentionally keeping my head down slightly, as I could feel the burn on my cheeks blushing. "So, where exactly in Colorado are we going, Bekah?" He asked while grabbing the portable GPS system.

"I will get that set up, you just drive out to the highway and I'll let you know." I grabbed the GPS out of his hand, mine grazing over his. I immediately felt an instant spark shoot through my arm as I touched his. Thankfully, I turned my attention to the GPS. I let my dark brown hair fall to the side of my face and started entering information so he wouldn't notice the little smile that formed my lips.

CHAPTER 6

I was just itching to get out of that damn car! I could feel my anxiety sneaking up on me and the overwhelming desire to stand straight and stretch my body. I kept switching from one hip to another, crossing one leg and then crossing the other. I'd grab a handful of my long, brown hair and braid it, then release the braid and start all over again. I couldn't keep still. Gabe kept looking over at me. I could see him out the corner of my eye every time he glanced my way. It made me even more nervous and I started picking at my fingernails. "You okay over there, Bekah?" Gabe asked seeming a little worried about me.

"Yeah, I'm great," I said trying to sound enthusiastic, but I knew he wasn't buying it when I saw him look my way again. "Actually, Gabe, could we by chance take a pit stop? I'm not picky; we can stop at a gas station, a rest area or, on the side of the road for all I care. I just really need out of this damn car as quickly as possible. It's been like three hours!" I started clinching my hands together and my breathing quickened.

"Yeah, sure, there's a rest area just on up the highway about six miles. Can you make it a little bit farther? If not, then yeah, I can stop on the side of the road," Gabe explained.

I took a deep, relaxing breath and lowered the window a bit for some fresh air, feeling a little relieved it wasn't too far away, and said, "No, I'll be fine. I can make it six more miles." I just needed to keep repeating it in my mind and all would be good, as I gave a reassuring smile to Gabe.

I never really considered myself a claustrophobic person before, but as I'm thinking about it, I hadn't ever been in a car for this long. Normally, I didn't have to go track down ghost's living loved ones, and the few times I had, it was always in a town close by. Typically the family members came to us. I decided to consider myself fairly lucky that this was the first time I'd had to go so far. I lifted my head up a little bit so I could get some wind on me. The cool, crisp air rushing across my face and down my neck helped me calm my wrecking nerves, and before I realized it we were pulling into the rest area. Thank heavens!

I meandered around the grassy area and made my way inside a small brick building. It only contained a few bathroom stalls and some maps of the area, but it was enough to make my nerves calm. We both grabbed some snack food from the overpriced vending machines. As we made our way back to the car, I climbed in the passenger side and felt so much better. My body had quit fidgeting, my head quit aching, my muscles had been stretched and overall, I was feeling pretty good again.

As he drove back onto the highway, I looked over at Gabe and asked, "Do you remember when we first met?"

He responded like I was asking him to remind me, "Uh, yeah, do you?"

I smiled and said, "Well, of course, I was just wondering."

After a moment or two of silence, Gabe started in, "It was about two years ago. I really considered myself a bit of a freak back then, because I wouldn't acknowledge that I could see or talk to ghosts, so I went to your Uncle Cooper and he helped me understand my abilities."

A soft grin came across my face as I thought of Cooper, "Yeah, he was a pretty good teacher, wasn't he?"

Gabe continued, "I remember seeing you walk through the kitchen, poured yourself a glass of tea and your Uncle introduced us. You would barely speak to me and then rushed back to your room."

I corrected him, "I spoke to you; I said it was it was nice to meet you, and then went back to my room."

Gabe stated, "I didn't see you again very much until after your Uncle passed. I gave you my condolences at his funeral, and we kind of hit it off after that." My mind briefly thought again of my Uncle.

I sighed out loud and stated, "I really miss him. I miss our talks and his advice. Sometimes I wish he would've stuck around so I could at least see him from time to time."

Gabe agreed, "I know what you mean. He was a great guy." There was a few moments of silence between us.

Gabe glanced over at me once again, "My question is: why haven't we ever dated, Bekah?" he asked. That question pulled me out of my thoughts quickly.

I swiftly thought of some reason to give him, "Well, you know what they say, never mix business with pleasure." I was quite proud of myself for coming up with that one, hoping it would end that portion of the conversation.

"But you agree that dating me would be a pleasure?" Gabe said with small smirk and his sparkling eyes. So much for ending that conversation I thought to myself. Now, how was I going to answer that one?

"I'm sure it would be a pleasure, Gabe, if we weren't disagreeing about how to deal with a ghost or what shifts we take," I said as I twisted strands of hair in between my fingers.

"I think we should try it. A date when we get back, my treat and I decide where we go," he said smiling.

"Why do you get to decide?" I asked teasingly.

"Because you would just go to Del's Diner if you chose. You need to do something different, something out of the ordinary. Something that has nothing to do with work," he shot back.

"Oh, okay. Guess we'll see what you come up with, and I only go to Del's to check out any new ghosts," I added quietly, "and to see if my parents happen to show up."

Gabe looked a little more serious, "I'm sorry, Bekah. I understand what you're saying, but I'm just asking for one night. Agreed? We will put Joe on look-out for your parents."

I softly smiled back at Gabe and said, "Agreed."

The car got silent as Gabe continued driving the highway. I often wondered if my mom and dad were up in their heaven and happy. I never saw them after they died, and so many years have passed. I was starting to lose hope. Of course I didn't have my reading abilities when I was seven. Regardless, all those times I went to the diner, I was always hopeful that maybe they would be there. I asked my Uncle Cooper one time if he had ever seen them. He said he hadn't, and I was quite surprised considering the manner they were killed.

As we drove and drove the long, never-ending highway, I was ready to call it a day. Being stuck in a car took some getting used to. Thankfully, Gabe stopped about every two hours for stretch break. He continued driving, despite my offering to. A couple times I felt myself dozing off. Car rides always made me tired and I was having a hard time keeping my eyes open. Upon waking up from a little nap, I looked out in the distance and I saw a breathtaking scene. The mountains of Colorado just seemed to magically appear in the distance. They were so beautiful and awe-inspiring. I leaned forward on to the dash of the car, as if moving those few inches got me so much closer. I just stared at them, enthralled in their majesty.

"Awesome," Gabe stated.

"Yes, they are so beautiful!!" I replied.

"*Almost* the most beautiful thing I've ever seen." Gabe glanced at me. I gave a small smile while feeling a little embarrassed, but I quickly gave my attention back to the mountains.

CHAPTER 7

We finally made it to Boulder, Colorado and Gabe started looking for the first hotel he could find. He was so tired of driving, and we both longed to be anywhere but in that car. The mountains seemed to be all around us. Gabe pulled in to a bed and breakfast. It was a large Victorian style house, painted dark brown with maroon trim. It had walk-out balconies on the upstairs level, which probably gave beautiful mountain scenery. There were multiple cars parked around it, so I was hoping they still had a couple of rooms open.

We walked in the front door and were greeted by an older woman. She was about 5' 7" grayish-brown hair that was layered, showing beautiful waves. She was very outgoing and pleasant when she said, "Welcome to Belle's Breakfast Nook. I am Belle. Would you young, love birds like a room?" She smiled and winked at Gabe. "We have cable, breakfast is served at eight am and, of course, the view is unbelievable."

My jaw fell open and I tried to explain, "Oh, no. No, no, no. You have the wrong idea. We are...."

Gabe interrupted, "--loving the view. So yes, we will take one room, please. Can we pay by the day? We don't know how long we will be here."

Belle answered Gabe, "Oh sure, no problem."

"Wait a minute, Gabe. We need to talk real quick," I told him.

"Thank you so much, Belle. I can't wait to just relax on a nice, comfy bed," he replied to Belle and completely ignoring me.

"Well, that's perfect then! Our beds are all king-sized, heavy down, pillow-topped bedding, with multiple pillows for your comfort. And if you need anything extra, just holler for me," she said to Gabe as if I was nowhere around.

"Hello....Gabe?" I was starting to feel like I wasn't going to get a choice here. Neither one of them would even look at me. "Gabe!" I blurted out loudly. "Might we have a little chat? Please?"

"Excuse us for a moment, Belle," Gabe said with a playful smile.

We both walked a little ways from Belle. "What are you doing? I was planning on getting my own room," I explained.

Gabe looked at me puzzled, and almost smirking, he said, "Really? Oh, I guess I'm just trying to save us money. I mean, why pay for two separate rooms when we can share?"

Belle jumped in smiling and said, "By the way, we only have one room left."

Of course you do, I wanted to reply back to her. I also wanted to smack that sweet smile off her face. "It's settled then, we will take the room. Right, Bekah?" Gabe asked, but already had his mind made up.

"Oh, now you're asking me?" I questioned.

"Bekah, remember when we talked about that business and pleasure concept in the car? You really need to start focusing on the *pleasure* part of it. I promise everything will be fine. I don't bite,"

Gabe smiled and looked back at Belle. I swear I saw her wink at him again.

"Let's get you two inside your room then!" Belle blurted feeling a sense accomplishment. For all she knew Gabe could've been an ax murderer holding my captive and here she was encouraging him.

We walked our way up the stairs to room eight. We had an actual key to our room on a "Belle's" key chain. The room was nicely set up with one king-sized bed, beautiful wooden end tables on each side, and a large dining table in the corner. "Wait a minute, Belle. Do you have a room with two standard beds, by chance?" It's one thing to share a room, but seriously, couldn't we get separate beds?

"Nope, like I told you, only one room left," she replied as she left and shut the door behind her.

I immediately sat my luggage down and headed towards the balcony. Two old fashioned French doors opened to a large, wooden balcony with a small table and two chairs pushed to the side. The mountains were in the distance, looking so majestic, with clouds hovering the tops of them. Gabe stepped out to enjoy the view. "We could eat dinner out here," he said smiling.

"We will relax this evening, but tomorrow we have to find Hank's wife and get things settled. And, yes, we could have dinner out here," I said, smiling inside and thinking how wonderful it would to eat with Gabe and the beautiful scenery. Of course, my nerves took over and as I turned to walk back inside, something caught my attention. In the corner of the balcony I swear I saw some purple fog swirling around, only momentarily, and then it was gone. "Did you see that Gabe?" I asked curiously.

"See what?" he asked looking around.

"Nothing...I guess. I'm probably tired from the long drive." I justified to myself.

I started unpacking and placing things where they were easiest to find. "What are you hungry for, Bekah? Mexican, Chinese...you pick." Gabe had the local restaurant menus.

"Hmm, how 'bout pizza? It's simple and easy cleanup," I suggested.

Gabe handed me the menus and said, "Ok, I'm good with whatever you pick. Would you mind ordering? I'm going to jump in the shower real quick."

I grabbed the menus and the phone to see what I find when I glanced up, seeing Gabe taking off his shirt. Oh, hell. His chest muscles seemed to be sculpted from stone and his abs were nicely defined against his beautifully bronzed skin. As badly as I wanted to remove my eyes, I just couldn't focus enough to do so. "Damn," I whispered out loud, not even realizing the word escaped my lips.

"What, Bekah?" he asked and looked at me with his amazing smile across his face. I finally looked away as I realized my face was changing to a shade of red.

"Nothing, I'm just ordering pizza," I replied as I turned my back to him. I had to get him out of my line of sight.

Now, don't get me wrong, I'd been on plenty of dates with guys, but none of them had been very serious. I seemed to be pretty good at pushing people away or finding flaws in them, but I have to admit that I was having a hard time in finding any flaws with Gabe.

I heard the shower running and ordered a large pepperoni and black olive pizza. I sat on the bed, telling myself to get with it and took a few deep breaths. I never, in a million years, thought this trip would mean sharing rooms and watching Gabe prance around half naked. It wasn't a bad thought, just an unexpected one that I wasn't quite ready to confront.

I heard the shower turn off and purposely kept my back facing the door so I wouldn't see him come out. The pizza hadn't arrived yet, so I had nothing to occupy my time. I figured it was my turn for the bathroom. I grabbed some pajamas shorts and tank top, but just as I turned to put them on the bed, Gabe walked out of the bathroom.

Steam was rolling all around him, his skin was wet and shimmering, hair thrown around on his head lying messily. Hot damn! Did he need to come out in only a pair of boxer shorts? I mean, would a shirt kill him? My eyes ran up and down his body while I was telling myself to look away. His tanned skin was glimmering from the water and beading down his chest. "I see you looking at me," Gabe said slyly. "If you stare any longer you're going to give me a complex." I quickly turned away, reached down to grab my clothes, and then felt his arms slide beneath mine and around my waist.

"What are you doing?" I asked him with a bit of a quivering voice.

"I'm just standing here. What are you doing, Bekah?" he said nonchalantly.

As I grabbed his hands to remove them, I stated, "I'm taking my turn in the bathroom. Pizza should be here soon. It's already paid for so..." I walked away quickly from his arms and accelerated my pace to the bathroom.

I shut the door behind me and slid myself down it and onto the floor. I sat on my butt, leaning against it. I drew my knees up to my chest and, again, just breathed for a bit. What was going on with me? I didn't usually go into dumbass mode just because I was around a hot guy. Of course, I didn't usually parade around a hotel room with a half-naked, hot guy either. This was Gabe, though. I mean, I'd been working with him for a year now and I always thought he was cute, but this was getting way beyond simply thinking he was cute. "Are you okay in there, Bekah?" Gabe called through the door and yanking me out of my trance. How long had I been sitting here thinking? "Pizza's here!" I hadn't even made it in the damn shower yet.

"Ok, be out soon!" I hollered back, thinking to myself that I had to get my emotions under control and stop freaking.

Clean and rejuvenated, I got dressed, combed my wet hair and headed out of the bathroom to grab a slice of pizza and relax on the bed. I threw my clothes in a plastic bag and tossed it by my luggage. Heading over to the table where the pizza was, I noticed Gabe just sitting there, not eating. "Why aren't you eating, Gabe? I get something you don't like?" I asked.

"No, I'm just waiting for you. Hell, I thought maybe you fell asleep in there. I was debating on rushing in to check on you," he grinned and reached for the pizza.

"Oh, I'm quite fine, Gabe. Eat your pizza," I replied back, reached over, grabbed myself a slice, and sat in the chair across from his. "So, what exactly are the sleeping arrangements?" I asked in between bites.

"What do you mean? There's a bed with lots of blankets and fluffy pillows, so I'm thinking we are sleeping there." He laughed out loud. I was starting to think Gabe found it amusing to see me uncomfortable. I finished my pizza, walked to the side of the bed, and pulled back the covers. Then I walked to the other side of the bed and pulled back only the top cover.

I looked at him with my eye brows raised and slyly smiling, "There, you sleep on this side and I will sleep on that side with a blanket in between us. Perfect!" I headed to the bathroom to brush my teeth real quick, and upon returning I noticed all the blankets were pulled back on the bed...both sides.

"I get cold at night," I heard Gabe whimper.

"Are you serious, Gabe?" I asked back.

"Damn, Bekah, will you chill? I'm not going to do anything horrible. You ought to know me better than that. Why can't you ever just relax and stop thinking?" Gabe replied.

"I can stop thinking...and I can relax. Fine, I'm going to lie down and watch a little television before I go to sleep." I slid into the bed and tucked the blankets under my side between Gabe and me. My nerves were not calming down.

"Sweet, what are we watching?" Gabe asked as he turned over and pulled all the cover between us loose again.

"Umm, I don't care. I really don't pay attention to it..."

"Because you just sit there and think?" Gabe said, thinking he was proving a point, as he reached for the remote.

"No, because I'm relaxing my mind, and winding down, and no, you can't have the remote!" I snickered at him.

The next thing I knew, Gabe grabbed just above my right knee and squeezed. I screamed, laughed out loud and yelled at him, "Stop, stop, stop! I'm really ticklish there! Here, you can have the remote!" I tossed the remote at him and poked him in the ribs.

"Oh, well, how 'bout here?" Gabe tossed back the covers and started grabbing my thighs. I kicked at him and he sat on my legs. I started hitting him and grabbing at his hands to get him to stop, all the while I was laughing and squirming.

"Fine!" I yelled at him, making my face as serious as I could. He stopped, looked at me with concern, and pulled his hands up to his head like I had a gun pointing at him.

He started to say, "Bekah, I'm…" and I shoved both my hands into his rib cage and started tickling him.

"How do you like it, Gabe?" I kept hollering at him. His laugh was intoxicating, his smile was absolutely charming. Right when I let go of his ribs, he reached over and grabbed me by my arms, threw me on my back and sat across my stomach while pinning my arms down against the bed. I could feel the sparks of electricity flitting from each of us as we touched.

"How do you like it, Bekah?" he said so innocently.

"I'm actually quite comfortable at the moment." I smiled at him.

He lowered his face to my neck, whispering in my ear, "Are you still comfortable?"

"Um, yes, if you ignore the fact my hands are going to sleep from your grip on my wrists." Gabe loosened his grip and lightly kissed my neck. His lips were soft and the kisses tickled my sensitive skin. A quick giggle escaped my mouth, and he came face to face with me, his lips just barely touching mine.

"Are you *still* comfortable?" His eyes were sparkling, his smile showed those cute dimples and sparks of electricity were running up and down my body. I had no idea how to answer. My mind was drawing a blank as I stared at him. He released his fingers from my left wrist, traced them down my arm and stopped gently at my face, his hand cupping my cheek ever so softly. He touched his lips to mine. He kissed me passionately and gently bit my lower lip. I felt his tongue trace my lips and I parted them to allow both our tongues to intertwine. His kisses became more passionate and my breathing was speeding up. I felt like I was going to suffocate and said, "Gabe..."

"Please don't tell me to stop, Bekah," he whispered and started lightly kissing down my cheek and to my neck.

"I just don't want you to think I'm the type of girl who has one night stands with any guy," I said softly, taking a deep breath to calm my nerves.

Gabe sat up and looked at me puzzled, "You think I'm that type of guy? One who just goes around sleeping with women and no emotional attachment or meaning to it? I thought you knew me better than that, Bekah." Gabe moved and sat at the end of the bed. "I've been trying for a year now to get you to go out to dinner with me, to go do something fun, or just make a connection but damn, you are a hard girl to get through. You can give a guy one chance, can't ya?" Gabe continued to sitting on the bed, running his hands through his hair out of frustration.

"I don't think that about you at all, Gabe" I said with complete honesty. I crawled across the bed and sat behind him. "I know I push people away, always find some reason as to why I can't go out, or ignore the feelings I have, but I will do my best not to ignore them...if you are good with that," I said and lightly kissed the back of his neck.

Gabe turned and climbed into the bed, covered up and said, "Bekah, you don't have to make deals with me or talk me into anything. I know what I want. It's you who needs to decide what you want. Come on," he smiled and gently kissed my forehead, "lie down and get some sleep; got a long day tomorrow."

Great, now I felt like a total idiot. I did like Gabe. Hell, I thought about him all the time. I grabbed the covers and turned over with my back facing him. I told myself to stop thinking about it, and just sleep. I always seemed to screw things up with guys, always over-analyzing situations and then pushing myself away from them. As I was lying, I felt Gabe wrap his arm around my waist and he whispered, "I don't give up that easily. Night, Bekah." I took a deep breath in, and felt so safe wrapped in his arm. It was the first time in a long time I fell asleep without thinking about my parents, my Uncle, or anything else, except Gabe.

CHAPTER 8

I awoke the next morning finding myself nestled next to Gabe with my face huddled against the nape of his neck. I savored the feeling of being close to him and the warmth that radiated off his body, keeping me warm. Then, dragging myself away, I quietly slid myself out of the bed, grabbed some clean clothes, and headed to the bathroom. As I crossed in front of the bed, I heard Gabe say, "Where do you think you are going?" I looked over to see him grinning.

"I'm going to go get dressed. You want to go have breakfast down stairs with me? Or would you rather I bring something up?" I smiled back at him, awaiting his response.

"I will get ready and go with you. Did you sleep well last night?" he asked climbing out of bed.

"Better than I ever have before." Now I couldn't stop smiling. "You are quite comfy to sleep next to."

"Well, maybe we can do it again real soon." Gabe grabbed his clothes and raced to the bathroom. "I'm first!"

"Hey!" I yelled back while starting to chase him, but he stopped right before the door and I ran smack into his back. I quickly stepped back, laughing; feeling a little embarrassed and said, "You kind of deserved that." I kept laughing out loud.

Gabe stepped to the side and motioned for me to enter, "It's all yours."

I went to step through the doorway and he threw his arm across it, "But there's an entry fee. Um, I think one kiss would suffice," he said with a sneaky smile on his face.

"Well, I think I can handle that." I took one step forward and lifted my face to his. Kissing his lips, I ran my fingers through his hair and down his neck. I felt the small tings of electrical spark race through my lips. "Good enough to enter?" I asked.

"No, I think you should try again." He attempted to keep his face serious, but wasn't doing a very good job. He lowered his arm and I entered the bathroom, keeping my eyes gazing straight at his. I shut the bathroom door and our gaze broke.

We went downstairs to the dining area and we both picked out our breakfast. It was a quaint, little breakfast nook with four small tables and two chairs at each one. Belle was in and out of the area, replacing coffee or adding bagels to the basket. I grabbed some cranberry juice to go with my bagel, and joined Gabe at the table. It was pretty quiet while we ate. Finally I broke the silence, "So, what do you think we should say to Hank's wife?"

"Tell her the truth; tell her who we are, and why we are here. Hopefully, she will just explain her reasons, and we will be off." He swallowed a gulp of orange juice and continued eating his plate of biscuits and gravy.

"Okay, guess we'll give it a try," I agreed.

We finished our breakfast and headed back upstairs to snatch the car keys. I made sure we had our room keys and the information Hank gave us on his wife. Gabe led the way out to the car, and I climbed in the passenger side after he opened my door. I smiled at him and quietly said, "Thank you." He pulled out of the drive and we both took in the sites of the city.

I really didn't know what the hell was going on with us. Were we dating? Were we still just friends? Were we...oh, hell, and here I go thinking about things again. Gabe made it sound so easy to simply take a step back and enjoy things. It was a whole new way of thinking for me. I decided I would try to work on it, but I doubted if I would ever just completely change the way I thought.

I grabbed the GPS and entered the address we needed to find. Gabe drove to an area of the city that housed very nice, and what looked like very nicely priced homes. It was a beautiful area, full of trees and perfectly mowed yards. Not one house had any objects out of place in the yards or any clutter on their porches. Gabe pulled into the drive of a stunning house with a red truck in the side driveway. I quickly thought about how we were going to confront this woman. I had to be delicate, as not to upset her by asking such personal questions.

We approached the house and rang the doorbell. Both of us stood there, waiting for an answer. "You talking, or am I?" I asked Gabe.

"You can," he quickly answered as the door opened.

A pretty woman who looked to be in her thirties stood in the doorway. She had long, straight, black hair and about the same height as myself. "Can I help you?" she asked politely.

"Hi, my name is Bekah. This is my co-worker, Gabe. Are you Cheryl?"

The woman nodded her head, "Yes."

"We were wondering if we could have a few moments of your time. No, we're not selling anything; just wanted to talk to you about your late husband, Hank." I really didn't know what else to say, so I tried making it as simple as I could.

The woman continued standing there, "Why? What do you need to know about my husband for?"

I replied, "I promise I will explain everything. May we come in for a little bit? It's kind of difficult to explain." Cheryl thought for a moment, held the door open, and stepped back so we could enter. I walked over to her couch and sat down. Gabe followed me and did the same. Cheryl stood in front of a wooden coffee table that was placed in front of the couch. "You might want to sit," I told her.

"No, I'm good. What's this about?" Cheryl asked, and I could see she was getting irritated.

"Have you ever heard of Ghost Readers?" I asked her.

She nodded her head yes and stated, "Who hasn't?"

I continued, "Well, that's good, so I don't really have to explain that part. We saw Hank. He's hanging out at a diner in Jasper, Iowa and he's angry. In an effort to calm him and bring him peace, I promised I would do something for him."

Cheryl's eyes started to glisten and I could see tears forming. "I miss him so much. Is he okay?

Why is he mad? What does he want?" Cheryl was becoming more and more filled with anxiety and regret.

"I don't want you to think I'm a judgmental person, for I am only here to bring solace to Hank, but he asked us to ask you: why did you go to another man?" My voice got softer and quieter with each word. I felt really embarrassed and completely wrong for asking. After all, it really wasn't any of my business.

"That's what Hank wants to know? He sent you all the way from Iowa to find out why I was with another man? That's typical. Why didn't he come with you? It's none of your business, really." Cheryl was clearly getting agitated.

"You're right," I quickly said, "it's none of my business and I wish I didn't have to be here. The unfortunate part of my Ghost Reading abilities is that I can see and talk to them. Hank is very determined to get a reason. Once he has it, I'm hoping it will give him understanding and he can pass on to his heaven. He really loves you, but he's filled with such anger and confusion, so he didn't trust himself to see you." I tried explaining the situation to Cheryl as gently as I could. Her eyes started tearing up again as I said Hank loved her. I felt very sorry and sad for her. She seemed emotionally filled with regret and remorse for what she had done.

Cheryl continued to pace in front of the coffee table. Gabe noticed a box of tissues and handed one to her. "Thank you," she said softly.

She took a deep breath and started speaking, "Hank was a good man. He had a big heart, a great sense of humor, and always took care of everything. That's why I married him. He could always make me laugh when I was down-spirited. We had three beautiful children that he loved very much." She took another breath and wiped her eyes with the tissue. "He became very successful in his construction business. He started working lots of hours and coming home very late. I would ask him to please slow down or stay home some days. Five-day work weeks turned into seven. Eight-hour days turned into fourteen. There were days I would beg him, but he always left. I felt like I rarely saw him. The bills were being paid and the kids had everything they needed, but I was lonely. I just wanted Hank." Cheryl was full on sobbing now. She stopped to catch her breath and wipe her face. "I just wanted my husband back, but I knew he wasn't going to give up on his career, even just a little bit. So, when I accidentally stirred the attention of another man, it was easy to replace my affections for him. It's not that I stopped loving Hank or didn't want to be his wife. I just wanted to not be lonely. He'll never forgive me. He'll stay angry forever over what I did." Cheryl was hysterical now, sobbing, sniffling, and though she tried to continue pacing, she sat down in a big, leather chair to help calm her. "And now I really am alone...completely alone. My children hate me and Hank is gone. I deserve it though." She was now tearing the tissues into small pieces as her breathed quivered.

I couldn't help but feel for her as she spoke. She looked so frail and empty. "Do you mind if I tell Hank this? Maybe if he hears it, he can find peace. I'm so sorry, Cheryl. It must be very hard on you. However, you have to find a way to forgive yourself, too."

Cheryl stood up reclaiming her composure, straightened out her blouse, and cleared her throat. "I will be fine. And no, I don't mind if you tell Hank, but I have no idea how he will react to it. I'm sorry you drove all the way here just to find me, but I do thank you for your kind concern toward my husband."

Gabe stood up, so I followed suit. I saw Gabe walk over to Cheryl and give her a warm-hearted hug. She cried a little bit more on his shoulder, then backed up and said, "Be safe on your return trip." We both headed for the door as she opened it and we left.

"So, thanks for all the help in there. You didn't say a word," I said to Gabe rather sarcastically as we headed to the car.

"What did you want me to say? You had it worked out. Besides, I gave her a tissue…and a hug. That was enough." Gabe responded, feeling rather proud of his contribution.

"Ok, well, that's done thankfully. When we heading back home?" I asked as I was really missing my house. I missed Del's Diner and my little office. I was not looking forward to the long drive though.

"Um, I thought we'd stay another night, and maybe head home tomorrow morning. However, Bekah, why didn't we just call Cheryl on the phone and talk to her? Did we really need to drive all the way here, not that I'm complaining, because it's been great," Gabe said as a smile spread across his lips.

"You think she would've told us any of what she just said if we called her? We probably wouldn't have made it past the Ghost Reader bit, much less received a real answer from her. Now, we know what to tell Hank," I explained to Gabe.

"That's why you are the boss," he replied.

We drove through town and Gabe stopped at a local Chinese restaurant. I got some Orange chicken and he got Sweet 'n' Sour, then we headed to the large Victorian house we were staying in.

We ate without saying much to each other. My mind was thinking about how I was going to explain everything to Hank. Occasionally, I would look up and see Gabe staring at me with a thoughtful look on his face. I finished up eating and threw away my trash.

It was just before noon and we had nothing else planned for the day. I turned on the television in search for something to watch. Hopefully a good movie was on. Gabe got up, threw his trash away, and grabbed the car keys. "You are going somewhere?" I wondered.

"Yeah, I'm going to scout the city, look around and see what there is to do. You want to go, or are you just going to lay there watching TV? Maybe we could go climb a mountain or hike?" Gabe face lit up while he waited for my answer. I could tell he was getting anxious to do something, but I really didn't feel like driving around town. I really wanted to just stay in and relax.

"Well, I was hoping you would want to watch a movie or something with me. If I go out with you now, will you watch one with me later? Maybe we can stop by a video store and see what's out." I always seemed to have to bargain with Gabe.

"Ok, you got a deal," Gabe replied with excitement in his eyes.

CHAPTER 9

Gabe and I had a great afternoon together. We stopped at a convenience store and bought a disposable camera. We went hiking through some woods and climbed large boulders. We drove up a big mountain and the view was breath taking. I took pictures of Gabe as he climbed up large rocks and acted like he was falling off. He was laying on a huge flat rock when he waved me over. "Lay down by me and give me the camera." I went over to him, handed him the camera, and laid down on the big rock next to him. He held the camera out and took several pictures of us together. He kept scooting closer to me and taking different pictures at different angles to make sure he got us both in.

We both laid there for a while, enjoying the clouds in the sky and the sun shining on us. "It's really beautiful here. I'm glad you drug me out of that hotel room," I told him. Gabe looked at me and smiled.

"I agree," he replied. I savored the time, emptied my mind of all thinking and simply let myself enjoy the moment.

We both must have both fallen asleep in the warm sun because I woke up to Gabe gently rubbing my arm saying, "Bekah, we must've dozed off, but I don't think napping on this big rock is a good idea. Hate for either of us to fall." He helped me up and we walked back to the car. The sun was going down and the air was getting chillier.

We made it back to the Victorian house after deciding it would be easier to see if any good movies were playing on cable. We both snuggled up on the bed and I started flipping through channels. We watched "The Notebook", which was fine with me because I am always up for a good love story. I was pretty certain Gabe had fallen asleep half way through, as I heard his steady, rhythmic breathing and an occasional light snore.

I reached over and pulled the covers back and took a sharp inhale, as I saw the same purple mist from earlier dissipating in the air. Gabe was still sleeping so I didn't see reason to wake him as the mist had disappeared. What the heck was that I thought? Did Belle have some kind of room deodorizer that automatically refreshed the room? Paying no further attention I climbed out of bed, grabbed my night clothes, and went to the bathroom to do my usual routine.

When I came back out and slipped under the blankets, Gabe woke up and he did the same. After he returned, I rolled over and put my arm around him. He was so warm, his skin soft and smooth. I started running my fingers up and down his back, stopping every now and then to run them through his soft hair. My fingers felt the small spark of electricity with every touch they made. I lightly kissed his upper back and shoulders. Gabe rolled over to his back and I laid my chin on his chest, looking into his eyes. He asked, "What are you doing, Bekah?"

"Nothing, just laying here going to sleep. Got to get up early to leave for home, right?" I smiled at him.

"Well, you're not getting much sleep when you're playing with my hair; not that I'm complaining," he smiled back.

"Fine," I said as I turned my head and laid it on his chest, "I will go to sleep then." I rested there as I felt his chest rise and fall from breathing. After about a minute I found my fingers, once again, making their way up and down Gabe's chest, tracing the lines of his muscles from his clavicle down to his belly button.

"Are you trying to seduce me, Bekah? 'Cause if so, it's working," Gabe said in a low voice. I continued what I was doing; enjoying the feel of his chest and abs. Gabe sat up slightly, rolled over toward me and kissed me passionately. He moved down to my neck while his hands slipped under my top, caressing my stomach. With every touch of his fingers, I felt the sparks of electricity run across my skin. He came back up to my lips and said, "You know what this is going to lead to, right, Bekah?"

"Must you always ask questions? Take your own advice and just stop thinking. I'm pretty certain I know where things will lead," I whispered to him as a smile grew across my face. I pulled his head down to mine and kissed him back. I felt his hands all over my body as he removed my tank top. I felt like I was being pleasantly electrocuted by his touch. I knew exactly what we were going to do and I wasn't stopping to think about it.

The next morning Gabe had loaded the entire luggage and brought me breakfast. He slinked his way back under the covers. We both ate fresh strawberries and bagels as he glanced at me several times, but neither of us said much. It did seem rather awkward having him next to me. He was my best friend and co-worker for a year and I was having a little trouble figuring out how I should act.

The car ride wasn't any better. Neither of us really knew what to say to each other. I could tell Gabe was feeling the same way. I glanced often to the rear view mirror to watch the mountains slowly disappear. "Is everything ok, Gabe? You are awfully quiet," I asked him.

"I'm fine, you?" He quickly said back. His face didn't look fine, though. He seemed like he was full of thoughts.

"I'm good. Ready to get home, but you seem like you are thinking of something. Do you regret last night?" I tossed the question out before I lost the courage to. I wanted to see how he would react.

"Last night? Oh, no," he said smiling, "I absolutely do not regret that at all. Why, do you?" Now he seemed to be working around whatever he was thinking about.

"No, I don't. It's nice not to think sometimes." I still wasn't convinced he was fine though. He wasn't his usual smiling and flirtatious self.

"So, if you were to think, what are we? Was that just some casual fling or do you consider us a couple?" he asked very seriously.

"I told you, I don't do casual flings. So, yes, I was hoping we were. I will admit, though, it seems different between us. Am I over thinking things again?" I said to him.

Gabe grabbed my hand, gently caressed it and said with a laugh, "You always over think. However, I really like it when you don't."

The drive home seemed to take even longer than the drive there. Maybe it was the anticipation of getting back home. At least Gabe and I were talking like normal again. We stopped periodically for gas and food. Any silence between us allowed me to think about how I was going to explain to Hank what his wife said. I would occasionally look over at Gabe, and he would smile at me. I thought of how I missed my talks with Joe, and made a mental note to go see him as soon as we arrived back to town. I thought about Walter, but couldn't really decide if I missed him or not.

Miles rolled by and hours ticked away until we finally reached our little town of Jasper. It was late I realized Del's would be closed, so we went straight to Gabe's house to drop him and his luggage off. We headed into the house; it was dark and very quiet. I felt Gabe's arms go around my waist then he whispered in my ear, "You could stay the night with me tonight. And before you say anything, there's nothing at your house that requires your dire attention that can't wait until morning." He gently pulled my hair back and kissed my neck.

"Well, you don't make it easy to refuse, do you?" I laughed and turned around to give my approval of staying the night with a kiss.

The next morning I awoke early, about five am. I quietly climbed out of bed and gathered my things. I didn't see any point in waking Gabe up, so I wrote him a quick note:

Gabe,
Woke up early .Going to the diner to see Joe.
Had a great night. See you soon.

I went into the diner and saw Joe sitting in his usual spot. "You're back!" He hollered across the room.

"Yes, I am. I missed you, Joe. How are things going?" I bellowed back as I was walking towards him. I slipped into the booth seat across from him.

"Not much going on here. It's been pretty quiet since you left. Hank is still fuming a bit though. You find out anything?" he asked.

"Yeah, I just hope it will be enough for Hank," I said back.

"Where's the pretty boy?" Walter quickly sassed behind me.

"Assuming you mean Gabe, he's at home sleeping, Walter. Why? Did you miss us?" I said with a smile.

He groaned, "Humph, hell no, I didn't."

"Well, I missed you; going so long without your cheerful disposition caused me such heartache," I said without even looking at him.

I ordered some breakfast from Deon and waited for my food.

"Do you live here Deon? You're always working," I asked teasingly.

"Sugar, my kids are all grown up," she said with a southern accent, "and I've got nowhere else to be, so I might as well be here." She walked away and yelled my order back to the kitchen.

I was talking to Joe about my trip when the front door chimes sounded. I really didn't pay attention to who came in, as my back was to them. I heard a familiar voice come from right beside me, "So you couldn't have at least woke me to say you were leaving?" Gabe sounded a little annoyed.

"Um, I left you a note. Didn't you find it?" I replied back.

"Yes, a lovely little 'see ya later' note. Nice, Bekah," he spouted. Gabe turned and walked towards the door again.

"Hey, wait up," I said, getting up and walking after him. "I didn't want to wake you. You drove all the way back and were exhausted. It's not like I was never going to speak to you again. Don't be jerk about it," I said, as I was the one getting irritated now. I was trying to think of him and let him sleep, but instead he came in angry at me.

"Yeah, pretty boy, don't get your panties in a wad." Walter had to throw that comment out.

"Shut up, Walter! I don't need your damn comments now!" Gabe yelled back at him. Walter chuckled to himself, quite amused by Gabe's anger.

"Hey! That's not necessary, Gabe," I said as I grabbed his arm and walked outside with him. "I have a phone; you could've just called me if you were going to be an ass!"

"An ass? You...oh, forget it. Go eat your breakfast. I'm going home." Gabe turned and walked away down the side walk. I let him go. Obviously, he was mad and needed to cool down. I wasn't going to keep chasing after him. I went back inside and found my food waiting on my table.

I slid in the booth once again. "Damn, you guys are so temperamental," I said to Joe.

"Oh, he will calm down, Bekah. Give him time," Joe replied and continued, "So, I take it you two are dating now?"

I looked up at Joe and considered his question, "Um, well, we were, yeah. I mean, yes, we are. Oh hell, Joe, I don't know. Last I knew we were, so there ya go." I thought we were still dating, but Gabe was angry when he walked away, so now I wasn't really sure. I decided to work on my new frame of thinking and just let it go for now.

I finished eating my food and looked around for Hank. I said his name out loud, hoping he would show himself, but nothing resulted. I went back to the big walk-in freezer where he would occasionally hang out, but still had no sight of him. I quietly said, "Ok, Hank, I will come back tomorrow." I have no idea if he heard me, but at least if he did, he would know I was ready to speak to him.

CHAPTER 10

I was so happy to pull into my driveway. I hurried to get my luggage and headed into the house. The familiar smells around me, the quietness of the woods, and being back in my drama-free house helped me relax. I had no plans for the day but to stay home. Technically, today was Thursday, and I probably should have gone to the office, but it had been a long week, so I decided that I needed the day off. After I put away the things from my trip, I started a steaming hot bath.

I threw my long hair into a messy bun, slipped out of my clothes, and slid in to the bathtub. The hot water swirled around my body leaving my muscles relaxed. I leaned my head back and let the worries of Gabe and Hank wander from my mind. I found myself thinking back to the Colorado trip and my nights with Gabe. A smile formed on my face as I thought. However, I could feel myself starting to think about what happened this morning at Del's, so I made myself stop.

I must've drifted into a sleep, because I woke up freezing cold. The water in the tub had cooled and I was shriveling up like a raisin all over. I quickly threw some water on my face to wake myself up and climbed out. I tossed on some grey sweat pants and a teal tank top, and then meandered to my bedroom. My phone was sitting on the bed and I noticed that it was blinking. I opened it and had one text from Gabe.

Sorry for bein jerk. Call me sometime.

Well, at least we were on talking terms again. I closed it and made a mental note to call him this evening.

The rest of the day seemed to fly by. I hadn't really been productive at all. I made a grilled cheese sandwich and a can of potato soup for dinner and then called Gabe. He answered quickly after the first ring. "About time," he said.

"Well, hello to you, too," I responded.

"I'm just giving you a hard time. What are you doing?" he asked.

"Absolutely nothing, and really enjoying it...you?" I asked.

"Same thing, but I'd rather be doing nothing with you. Care if I come over for a bit?" He sounded kind of bummed.

"I don't care. I'm going to put in a movie. See you soon?" I replied.

"Great," he said before he hung up the phone. I went to pick out a movie, but thought I'd wait until Gabe came so he could choose. I usually tend to pick the love stories or romantic comedies and I knew Gabe like the horror and science fiction movies.

The minutes rolled into hours and Gabe never showed. I ended up watching television as I waited for him. I was a little irritated. I mean, why ask to come over and then not show? Not even call me to let me know? Men! This is why I hated dating, so damn confusing all the time.

Are you standing me up? I texted him.

No response.

Well, I'm not waiting any longer

Still no response.

I grabbed "*Footloose*" movie, put it the DVD player, and then climbed into my bed. Snuggling up inside my warm blankets and with pillows all around me, I could feel my eyes getting heavy and staying shut longer with each blink.

I opened my eyes briefly to try and continue to watch the movie, but very quietly I heard a noise outside. Well, I thought I did. I lazily scanned the bedroom and my eyes stopped at the window. I quickly jumped out of bed and ran to it; slamming the window open, I looked outside. I had to have been losing it. Maybe I was just really tired, because I swear I saw a set of purple glowing eyes looking at me through the window. Nothing was outside, just the sound of crickets and bugs in the night. I didn't see anything moving and the wind was very still. After shutting my window I headed back to my bed. Quickly, I wrote it off in my head, deciding that I must've been half-dreaming. I climbed back into bed and allowed myself to enter a slumber.

The dream, or shall I say nightmare, was horrendous. I woke up in a sweat with tears running down my cheeks, trying to remember what the nightmare was about. All I could see in my head were images of Gabe being beaten, bloody, and half dead. I looked over at my clock and it was just after three am.

I tossed the blankets back, sat on the edge of the bed, and drew in a deep breath. "It was only a nightmare", I repeated out loud to myself. I stared down at the floor and after collecting myself, stood up to go to the bathroom. As I stood, I quickly looked up towards my doorway. I had this really creepy feeling that I was being watched. I looked all around the room, my breath becoming more frantic, and then quickly I turned the light on. I didn't see anyone or anything. I glanced towards my window and nothing seemed out of place. Maybe I was just letting my paranoia get to me. After all I did just have an odd dream. I've lived alone for quite a while now and I've never let the odd noises get to me before. My breathing slowed and I proceeded to the bathroom.

I couldn't get rid of this feeling, though. It gnawed at my mind until I decided I had to do something to relieve it. I headed to the front door and locked the deadbolt, then locked the back sliding door. I checked a few windows, but then I thought that maybe I was being a little over dramatic. It was possible that maybe the nightmare was making me more on edge than usual. I grabbed my phone to see if Gabe ever wrote back; still nothing. I made my way back to my room and climbed back in bed.

Awaking around seven am, I went into my office. I was going to try and talk to Hank today. I also wanted to see Gabe and ask where in the hell he was last night. When I got to the office, it was already open and Gabe was sitting at his desk. "Hey," he said as he came close and kissed my cheek.

"Hey? That's it? Just hey? Why didn't you make it over last night, Gabe?" I asked him. "I texted you a couple of times and you never responded. I waited hours for you."

"Yeah, I guess I was really tired," Gabe continued, looking rather exhausted. "I'm sorry, Bekah. I was out like a light and didn't even hear my phone go off. I noticed it this morning, but I figured I'd have some explaining to do, so I just waited for you to get here. I did, however, stop to get your usual." Gabe smiled and pointed to my desk. There was my cappuccino and danish.

"Thank you," I said and looked at him with concern. "Are you okay, Gabe? For sleeping all night, you look rather tired." Gabe seemed to be pale, his eyes were dim, and he wasn't as perky as usual. Gabe had always been a happy morning person, but today he just looked gauntly. Gabe and I differed in that area as I was a horrible morning person. After I had about thirty minutes to wake myself up I became more tolerable.

"I'm fine. Guess I'm just recovering from the long drive. I really am sorry for not showing last night. Can we try it again? I will make it up to you," he said trying to convince me.

"Sure, but why don't you come with me to see Hank? Then you can go home and rest. It's Friday, so we have all weekend." I smiled at him.

He smiled back and winked at me, "Sounds good, thanks."

We headed to the diner and after we arrived, I immediately started searching for Hank. That ghost was never around when I wanted him. Gabe and I sat at a table while we kept an eye out for him. Walter was across the diner, looking at us. I could tell he was just waiting for his moment.

"Hi, Walter," I said cheerfully.

"Humph," he responded in his usual way.

I thought I'd try my luck a little with him so I asked, "Are you ever happy, Walter?"

He furrowed his brow and replied, "Happy? Well, yeah, I'm happy all the time. What the hell makes you ask that?"

"Nothing," I quickly responded as I spotted a red aura toward the back of diner.

"Found him. Follow me," I quietly said to Gabe.

We reached the back door and Hank was pacing as he usually did just outside the diner. He saw us and kept pacing. I said, "Hank, I was here yesterday to speak with you, but I couldn't find you. Are you ok?" Hank continued to pace. He didn't seem worse than when we left, but he didn't seem any better, either.

"I wasn't sure I wanted to hear what you had to say, so I stayed away. I knew you'd be coming back today, though; so, here I am. What did my wife say?" Hank was obviously stressed out.

"It would be better if you would let me in your head, then I will explain it and help you find peace. Are you okay with that?" I asked, not really expecting him to allow it.

"Well, the last time I said no, you did it anyway, so fine. Do what you have to do." He seemed eager to find out information.

"Okay, I'm just going to pat you on the shoulder," I warned him, so he wouldn't be caught off guard.

I touched his shoulder, and immediately felt the spiral feeling of being on a roller coaster. I started seeing the images of how he died and immediately shoved them away. I started talking to Hank. "Your wife is very lovely. She misses you," I said to him.

"Get to it, girl," he responded. I was hoping to calm him, but that obviously wasn't the way to do it.

"Okay, well, here it goes. Your wife loved you with all her heart, but she was lonely, Hank. You put all your time into your work and left none for her. When she went to another man, it wasn't because she didn't love you or want to be your wife; it was simply because she needed attention that you wouldn't give." As I spoke, I used my mind to help decrease the anger in his. I sent positive thoughts, happy ideas, and waves of glee in an attempt to help his mind release some anger. "She misses you terribly. She regrets everything, but knows nothing will bring you back. She is very lonely," I spoke, but continued shoving happiness waves into his brain.

I could see the redness of his aura dying down. It was more pinkish-white tinged with a blue hue. His emotions were turning into sadness more than anger. I could feel his mind becoming depressed. I continued talking, "It wasn't your fault, Hank. She doesn't blame you or hate you. She wishes she could do it all over again, and do it differently, but that's impossible. Your death was tragic, but you have to come to terms with it."

I now started driving images of peace into his mind and channeled energy waves of tranquility and calmness, to help him find his way. I slipped out of his head and back into mine. I opened my eyes and dizziness overtook me. Gabe helped keep me steady and grabbed a chair for me to sit in.

"All ok, Bekah?" he asked.

"Yeah, I think so. The rest is up to him," I responded as I held my head in my hands, trying to regain equilibrium.

"Ok, that's fine, but I meant you. Are *you* ok?" he asked.

"Oh, yeah, you know how it is. I will be fine." I looked at Gabe and smiled. He still didn't look any better than before; his eyes were half open and his brow was furled. I sat there for a few minutes as the dizziness and nausea resolved. Hank was still lingering in the same spot; his aura now swirling a light blue color.

"Are you okay, Hank?" I asked him quietly.

"I will be," he responded just before he disappeared.

I stood up, grabbed Gabe's hand, and said, "Let's go, it's time for you to go home and relax. Try to get some sleep." We walked back to the office and Gabe gathered his things.

He was getting ready to walk out the door, when he turned and said, "You could always come with me, Bekah. I'd probably sleep much better with you by my side." He had that familiar flirtatious grin, although it this time it was more weary and pathetic looking. It still was enough to make it hard for me to say no.

"I will give you a ride home only because I don't want you walking. I could stay until you fall asleep, but then I will probably go home so I don't wake you. That okay?" Gabe nodded his head and I grabbed my stuff.

Gabe's house looked like hell. He hadn't put away anything from the trip. His kitchen had dirty dishes in the sink and other dishes sitting on the coffee table in the front room. His bedroom had clothes thrown all over the floor. Gabe is usually a very clean person and rarely was his house disarrayed. He saw me looking around the house in disbelief when he said, "I know, it's a mess. I'll clean it later. Come on." We walked into his bedroom. He threw himself on the unmade bed and waved for me to lie beside him. I crawled in next to him as he cuddled himself next to me and wrapped his arms around my waist. "Don't leave until I'm completely asleep...if you must leave, that is," he said quietly as he kissed my neck.

"I won't. Just sleep, Gabe," I said back as I ran my fingers through his hair. Gabe closed his tired eyes and quickly I noticed his rhythmic breathing begin.

I waited for a while, about an hour, I think, before I slid myself away from him. Gabe didn't even flinch, much less wake up. I closed the door to his room and began cleaning his house. I washed the dishes and picked up the front room, gathered all the clothes I could find, and tossed them into his washer. After the house was back to its usual state, I left Gabe a note and went back to the office.

I cleaned up my desk and arranged my files in order. I made a few phone calls to some family members waiting to hear back about their loved ones. A ghost couple, meaning man and wife, showed up and I spoke with them in regards to what they wanted resolved. They were both with blue auras so I knew it would be safe to do a reading. They both wanted the same thing, to inform their daughter they loved her and that they were okay.

It was getting late into the evening, so I stopped by the diner before heading home. I wanted to check on Hank and see how he was doing. Heading to my usual spot to sit, I waited to see if I could catch a glimpse of him. I had no idea if he was still around, but I was curious if he was doing any better. Walter walked in the aisle next to me, grumbling under his breath. I didn't even bother to ask what he was going on about.

I didn't see Hank anywhere, so I wandered to the back of the diner. Hank was there, sitting on the floor in front of the dishwasher. "How are you doing, Hank?" I asked knowing he was still a little sad.

"I'm ok, I guess. I'm still wrapping my head around things," he replied rather drearily. I felt bad for him. He wasn't a bad guy or horrible husband, he did what he felt was right at the time and shouldn't have been blaming himself.

"Think all you want, Hank, but no point in blaming yourself. What's done is done. Would you like me to re-enter your mind and help you find peace?" I asked him.

"No," he replied, "I will figure it out. Thank you anyways." I smiled compasionatelya t him and walked out the way I came.

"Boy still boo-hooing back there? My God, all he does is cry and whine all day. He needs to grow a pair!" Walter yelled at me as I approached the door. I knew Walter couldn't help himself from making just one comment, but at least it wasn't about Gabe.

"Thank you, Wal--" I tried to finish, but he interrupted me.

"And where's that lazy ass boyfriend of yours? Is he still mad at you and stomping around the place?" Of course, there it was.

"No, he isn't mad. He's at his house sleeping," I replied.

"Well, that's typical of most lazy asses," he remarked, knowing exactly what would irritate me.

"Sometimes, Walter, I wish you would just keep your rude comments to yourself. Good night!" I hollered back as I walked out the door.

CHAPTER 11

I thought about going back to check on Gabe, but I didn't want to wake him; he needed his sleep. After arriving home, I walked through my house, picking up things here and there, and then washed up in the bathroom as I always did before bed. I changed and then got comfy under my blankets as I switched on the television. I didn't really watch anything so I flipped it to the local news, using it once again as a way to distract my mind, allowing it easier for myself to wind down.

I awoke at about one am, and turned the television off. I rolled over in bed and went back to sleep. Again, nightmares flooded my mind.

I was in the small house where I had lived with my parents. I stood in front of the empty couch where they both had laid with bullet holes in their foreheads. Suddenly both of them appeared on the couch, dead. The blank expression upon my mother's face horrified me. She was so beautiful and I hated seeing her look so lifeless. My father's face had blood dripping down it and contained his blank, empty eyes. The same two pictures alternated constantly; first my mother, and then my father. The images were making me sick to my stomach. Just when I didn't think I could bear seeing the visions of my parents any longer, the dream changed to my Uncle Cooper. I was back at my house, standing in the front room. He sat at our dining room table. He was moving his mouth like he was talking, but I couldn't hear him. "Are you trying to say something, Uncle Coop?" I asked him. Again, he just moved his mouth inaudibly. I started walking closer to him, and he started to make more sense.

In a low whisper, I heard him say, "Don't trust him, Bekah. Don't trust him." He kept repeating it over and over.

"Don't trust who, Uncle Coop?" I asked him. He continued to repeat the same sentence. I walked away from him and headed to the front door of the house. I turned around to look at him and he had begun racing towards me, yelling, "DON'T TRUST HIM, BEKAH!" Uncle Cooper scared the hell out of me. My whole body jumped and I gave out a little scream. As soon as he said it, he was gone.

I opened my eyes and realized I was lying in bed, my tank top wet with sweat. I sat straight up, breathing heavy. I held my head in my hands as I tried to catch my breath. What was with these horrible dreams? They were making it impossible for me to sleep. I never wanted to even think about my mother's face again. The sooner I forgot about that dream, the better. And was it necessary for Uncle Cooper to scream at me? I don't ever recall having a hearing problem when we lived together.

I got out of bed and grabbed a new tank top from my dresser drawer. I pulled off the one I was wearing and put the new one on. I glanced across the room and, again, let out a small scream as I saw two glowing purple eyes in the doorway. I immediately took two steps back and continued staring at the mysterious eyes. Were those eyes? Was I seeing things? Why did I only see these after I woke up from a nightmare? I quickly rubbed my eyes and looked for them again, but they were gone. How long had they been there? I had just changed my clothes right in front of it! I walked across the bedroom and to the hallway, trying to find where the purple eyes were coming from. I got goose bumps from the chill in the air. I didn't see anything, but I did hear my front door slam shut. I ran across the house to the front door and opened it. Again, I didn't see anything. I listened as closely as I could, but it was quiet outside.

Back inside, I was starting to freak out. I locked all the doors and windows, then ran back to my room. I grabbed my phone and called Gabe. It rang and rang but no answer, only voice mail. I left a message asking him to call me as soon as he awoke. I noticed that my voice sounding a little frantic, but my mind was reeling from the possibility of someone being inside my home and watching me. I sent a text to him as well:

Please call me soon

There was no response from him, but I knew he was sleeping. I glanced at my clock, 4:17 a.m. I didn't feel right staying at home, although I knew the intruder had left; I heard the door shut. I convinced myself of my safety, as I had secured all the windows and doors, but I sure as hell wasn't able to go back to sleep.

I mostly stayed in my bedroom. I changed my bed sheets and cleaned out my dresser drawers, mainly because I didn't know what else to do and I felt the need to stay busy. I realized I kept looking all around me making sure there were no eyes peering at me. I didn't see any, of course, but that didn't stop me from constantly looking. Finally, at seven o'clock I had enough and decided to leave and go into town.

I didn't know where I was going, maybe Del's, maybe the office, or maybe to Gabe's. He ought to be waking up soon. I grabbed a pair of sweats and long sleeved tee, changed in my bathroom and I was out the door.

I made it to Gabe's house and knocked on the door. He didn't answer. I let myself in and peeked at him in his bedroom. He laid there in his mess of a bed. I gently climbed in next to him. He briefly awoke and said, "Hey, Bek. Take a nap with me." A nap? Hell, he had been sleeping for twelve hours. What did he need a nap for? I, however, hadn't been sleeping. I felt exhausted from being terrorized by nightmares and purple eyes.

"Okay," I whispered and cuddled up next to him, feeling safe in his arms.

Gabe wrapped his arms tighter around me and whispered, "I love you, Bek." It took me by surprise and I didn't know what to say in return. I wasn't even sure if he realized he said it. His breathing didn't change and he didn't move a muscle. I must admit, my heart skipped a beat and a smile instantly formed on my face. After running my fingers through his hair a few times, I closed my eyes and entered into a nice, uninterrupted sleep.

I woke up and stretched my arms over my head. I stopped mid-stretch as I looked around and quickly remembered I was at Gabe's house. I was alone in his bed, but I heard noises coming from the living room. I leapt from the bed and walked out to see Gabe sitting on the couch watching television. He stood up and got his coffee cup from the dining room table. He was wearing a pair of black and blue plaid boxers. That was it; no shirt, no socks, just boxers and damn he looked good in those boxers. Then, he sat back down, focusing on the news show. I walked across the room, and he turned to see me coming. He smiled big at me and said, "Good afternoon, Bek. Wondered when you would wake up." I glanced at his clock on the wall. It was 2:15 in the afternoon. Damn, I slept a lot longer than I had planned to.

"Hey, got anymore coffee?" I asked him. He jumped up and went into the kitchen. "I can get it, Gabe," I hollered to him, but he quickly returned with a cup. "Thanks," I said with a small smile. "You should've waked me earlier. I didn't mean to sleep that long."

"Bek, what happened last night? I got your voice message when I woke up and you sounded a little freaked out. Then, I read your text. I thought you stayed here. When did you leave?" he flicked off the television and faced me.

"I stayed for a little bit after you fell asleep, cleaned up your house, and then headed home. I went to bed, fell asleep, and woke up from a horrible nightmare. I saw someone staring at me in my bedroom, or I thought it was someone. I don't know, it freaked me out so I called you." I finished explaining the rest of the morning to him.

"So, did you actually see someone or just think you did?" he asked me, trying to understand what I was saying.

"Yes...well, no. Maybe, I'm really not sure. I know I heard my door shut. I stayed there as long as I could, but then I just had to leave. So I came here. I didn't know where else to go. I hope that was alright with you," I explained, or at least I thought I had explained. Hell, I was confusing myself.

"Of course, it's alright. You can always come here, Bek." He walked over and wrapped his arms around me, giving a hug. "Thanks for picking up my house, by the way. It was a total mess. I don't usually let it get that way."

I wrapped my arms around him and said, "I know. Are you feeling better? You asked me to take a nap with you when I climbed in your bed. Did you catch up on your sleep?" Gabe looked much better than he had the day before. His eyes were bright and maybe it was because he was walking around in only a pair of boxers, but nonetheless, he acted better, too.

"I don't even remember talking to you. Maybe I was a little sick and I slept it off, but yeah, I feel fine now. Got plenty of sleep, I think," he said, as he ran his fingers through my hair. Just being next to him in his arms, feeling his smooth skin made me smile. Gabe continued, "So, I do believe you owe me a date, my choosing of place." Right he was. I forgot about the date we had set up while we were in Colorado.

"Okay. Where and when?" I responded.

"You feel up to doing something tonight?" he continued running his fingers through my long hair.

"Sure, I'll just need to run home so I can change and such. I can meet you back here this evening if you want."

"Why don't I run you home, since you got a little freaked out? I will make sure everything is okay. Then, when you're ready, we can head out. As for where...I will let that be a surprise." His smile lit up his eyes, making them sparkle.

"Okey doke, but you know I really don't like surprises, so keep it simple, will ya?" I leaned in and kissed him on his lips. He pulled me closer and ran his hands down my neck, bringing them to rest on my shoulders. "We better go now then," I laughed and pushed him away to his room so he could get dressed.

CHAPTER 12

We made it to my house and Gabe went in first, searching around to ensure everything was safe. I kind of figured it was fine, but it made me feel better having him there. I went to my room and grabbed some clothes. I took a quick shower and when I was ready, I opened the door to find Gabe standing in the doorway. "So, can I stand here and stalk you?" he said laughing.

I smiled at him and said, "Well, I'd rather it be you than anyone else." I started laughing. "I'm ready when you are. Just let me lock up before we leave." I didn't want to take a chance that my house would be rummaged through while I was gone.

After locking up we both got in my car and Gabe drove back to town. "I have to pick a few things up, so you mind waiting for me at my house and I'll be back soon?" Gabe asked.

"Sure. What are you picking up?" I asked.

"That's for you to find out, now isn't it?" He smiled at me.

"Ok, I'll just go through all your personal belongings while I wait," I sassed back at him.

He dropped me off at his house, and after I entered the door, Gabe drove away. I plopped down on the couch and turned on the television. I flicked through the channels, wasting time until Gabe returned. I wondered where he would be taking me. Getting bored with the television I wandered around his house, made his bed that I helped mess up, and then looked at the pictures on his walls. There was one of him and his parents when he was younger. I really liked the picture of him and my Uncle Cooper standing side-by-side. I moved on and threw the clothes from the washer into the dryer. With nothing left to do, I plopped back down on the couch. I pulled out my cell phone and texted him:

So…hows it goin?

I patiently waited for his response.

Fine. On way back.

I smiled and went by the door to wait for him. Soon enough, I saw my SUV pull into his drive. I opened the front door and Gabe met me there. "Hi, I'm back," he said and smiled, while holding nothing.

"I noticed. Thought you were going to get something?" I asked.

"I did. You can't stand not knowing something, can you?" he joked and shut the door behind him.

"No, actually, I can't. So just tell me, what are we doing?" I asked again, grabbing his hand and pulling him back to the door. I felt like an impatient giddy school girl.

He laughed, "I take it you're ready to go then? We leave in about forty-five minutes. Perfect timing is essential," he said, then pulled me in close to him. He led me to the couch and said, "Have a seat, Bekah. I'll get you a drink while we wait to pass the time."

Gabe went into the kitchen, got two glasses, and poured half a cold beer into each one.

I usually don't drink, but I couldn't think of a reason not to, so I took the glass from him when he brought it over. It was ice cold, and felt good as I swallowed it down my throat. Between sips I asked Gabe, "How old were you in the picture with you and your parents?"

Gabe walked over to the wall and said, "I was sixteen years old and just got my driver's license. It's the only picture I have with them before they died." Gabe took another swallow.

"Oh, I'm sorry. I didn't mean to bring up sad memories," I said.

"You didn't. My dad was so happy I passed, he asked the woman at City Hall to take our pic. Guess he thought I'd flunk," he said, softly smiling at the memory.

"Did your parents know you could see and talk to ghosts?" I asked him, not knowing if it was a bad subject or not.

"No, for many years I pretended like I couldn't see them. I acted like they weren't there if they spoke to me, and I definitely didn't try to talk to them," Gabe explained. "When I was eighteen my parents died, and it was then I decided to look up your Uncle Cooper. He was well known at Del's for what he did, so he seemed appropriate to ask."

"I see. Did you ever see your parents?" I questioned.

"Yep, that's what made me go looking for Cooper. I saw them one last time before they moved on. They told me they loved me and would always look over me. They were both happy. I do miss them, though," Gabe finished off his drink and headed back to the couch.

"Well, at least you know they are happy; that's good," I said. More than what I know, I thought. I finished off my beer and took both our glasses into his kitchen. I returned to Gabe and sat next to him. He put his arm around my shoulders and pulled me close.

"It's odd how they always make their way to Del's, isn't it?" Gabe asked me. "I mean, some days our town is crawling with ghosts and other days, hardly any."

"Yeah, but Cooper told you why, right?" I asked and Gabe shook his head no.

"I never really thought to ask him," he said curiously.

"Well, we live here, on Earth, in Jasper. As you know above us is Heaven, and below us is Hell," I explained.

"Or that's what we were told, anyways," Gabe interjected.

"Yes, but that's what I believe, too," I continued. "Uncle explained it to me like this: the world as we know it has a blanket around it, sort of like a veil that separates our world from the heavens. However, in the spot of the blanket just over Jasper, it's more like a sheet. The veil is thinner here, and easier for ghosts to pass through. They sense it when they die and feel a tug to come here. Some can ignore the tug, others follow it. I have no idea if any other place exists like this."

"Did Cooper ever try to find any other place other than here?" Gabe asked.

"Not that I know of, but I never asked him either," I replied.

"Hmm, that's interesting. So, we help by feeding them positive energy waves, and they cross over where it's the easiest to pass," he said back.

"Yep, that's how I see it," I said. "So, how did you do it...ignore the ghosts? Did you just not respond to them or what?"

"Well," he explained, "it wasn't easy. Ghosts would show up at my house, follow me home from school and eventually would show up in my classroom. Usually I just walked away. It was more difficult at school though. I couldn't just walk out of class. The other kids thought I was a freak. Especially at the beginning because I didn't know what to do, so I would just cover my head up." He chuckled a little bit. "I mean, literally, cover my head with books or paper so I wouldn't have to look at them."

I laughed out loud. "What did your teachers do?"

"They'd uncover my head and when I wouldn't stop doing it they started taking my recess away, which meant I remained stuck with the ghosts in my classroom. Eventually I learned to just ignore them. I know it sounds silly, but I didn't have anyone to teach me. You were very lucky in the aspect that you had Cooper," Gabe continued with a smile, "and I was very lucky Cooper had you."

Gabe glanced outside and said, "It's time." He helped me up from the couch and caught me in his arms. He gave me a quick kiss and said, "Let's go."

Gabe led the way to my car. He drove to the outskirts of town in a way I rarely go. It was the opposite side of town from my house. It didn't take long before he pulled onto a gravel road and drove back into the woods. We came to a stop and he said, "Come on, Bekah. Follow me." He opened up the back door, took out a picnic basket and blanket, and then grabbed my hand to lead the way.

We walked for a few minutes through the wooded area and came to a clearing. It was just a circular clearing inside the forest of trees, filled with beautiful yellow and purple flowers. He picked two of them, smiled as he handed them to me, and my heart skipped a beat. He searched for a good spot and spread the blanket a part of inclined ground. We both sat as he opened the basket and pulled out two wine glasses and a bottle of wine. He pulled off the cork, and poured us both a glass. He, then, pulled out two bacon sandwiches and a bag of chips. He made us both a plate and placed mine in front of me. "How'd you find this place, Gabe? It's awesome!" I said enthusiastically.

"I know a few good places in this town that maybe other people don't know about. You like?" He asked.

"I love it. Thank you for bringing me here. But why did we have to wait? You drove straight here," I wondered. Gabe took the drink from my hand, and placed both glasses in the picnic basket for safe keeping.

He said, "Lie down on your back and look up to the sky and tree line." I lay back, and understood the reasoning for his timing. The sun had just gone down, and it was dusk. The beautiful colors of orange, red and yellow shined through the trees and onto the flowers. It made the whole place seem magical. "I used to come here when I wanted to get away from the ghosts that kept pestering me. It's nice and quiet," he said.

"Not to mention it's beautiful the way the last light from the sun shines through the trees and makes the flowers glow," I said with excitement.

"Yeah, but it's more beautiful tonight than I've ever seen," Gabe said and grabbed my hand as we both just laid there watching the field of glowing flowers.

We eventually sat up and ate our sandwiches while sipping on the wine. Occasionally, I picked up a chip and munched on it. "Where'd you get the food?" I asked.

Gabe just smiled and said, "Well, I've learned that you have to have a little bit of Del's in everything you do, so I had them made for us. They're pretty good," he said.

We finished our food and most of all the wine was gone. We both lay back again, staring now at the stars in the sky. Each one could be seen perfectly, no clouds in sight, and it was just a little chilly. I snuggled up next to Gabe to help keep me warm. He ran his fingers up and down my arm, occasionally tickling me. I giggled and had a hard time keeping the smile off my face. Gabe turned on his side and propped his head up with his hand. He looked utterly amazing in the night with the moonlight shining on him. He smiled, his eyes shined, and the butterflies in my stomach were doing complete flip-flops. He traced my face with his finger, and said in a soft, quiet voice, "You're so beautiful, Bekah. Thank you for my date."

He leaned over and kissed me. My mind went dizzy from the passion of his kiss, or maybe it was the wine, but either way it felt unbelievable. It wasn't that kind of dizzy feeling after leaving a ghost and I felt like I was going to puke, but that kind of light-headed feeling that made me feel like I was floating in the air. I wrapped my arms around him and kissed him back. I pulled at his shirt and removed it while I threw my leg up and flipped him over, so I was sitting on him. I gently kissed his neck and my fingers lightly played on his chest. I could hear the pounding of his heart as my lips grazed his chest. He gently grabbed me and rolled over, so he was now sitting on top of me, and as he softly nibbled at my earlobes he whispered, "My turn." This had to have been the best date ever.

CHAPTER 13

Daybreak had come with the morning sun shining down on us. I helped Gabe gather our stuff, and we walked back to my car. He drove us back to his house, and I assisted with putting away the things from our picnic. Gabe was going to jump in the shower and I told him I'd better get home to do the same. He was pretty insistent on going with me to make sure all was okay, but I assured him I would text or call if anything was wrong. "You can come out later, if you want," I said to him as I walked to the front door. "I'll make dinner." Gabe joined me at the door, and kissed me intensely. "However, I'm not going to want to leave if you keep that up," I smirked at him.

"Well, then don't," he said between kisses.

I took a step back and smiled at him, "Not going to stand me up? I will see you later then?"

"Absolutely! I will be there, Bek," he replied enthusiastically.

I was in complete dream land as I stopped at the grocery to buy some steaks for dinner and on the entire way home. I barely remembered the drive, as my thoughts were on the upcoming evening. Before even entering my house, I stopped at my flower bed and pulled out some weeds. I decided my lawn needed mowing. So after I placed the groceries in the fridge, I went to my shed and started up the riding mower. It was a beautiful day, and perfect for some lawn work. I worked outside most of the morning and into the early afternoon. When I was all finished and my yard looked great, I went inside, got a cold iced tea to drink, and turned on the shower.

I grabbed my phone and texted Gabe as I searched for some candles in the kitchen cabinet.

Had a great time last night. Can't wait 2 c u

My stomach was still flip-flopping and my heart quickened by just thinking of him. I wanted everything to be perfect. I put the candles on the table and went to the couch to relax a bit.

Me too. Im comn tonite rite? he replied.

Well that was the plan or did u 4get already I teased back. I mean, that was our plan.

No I b there. Shall I bring anything he responded.

Just yourself I texted back. I wanted to add 'in nothing but your boxers', but I didn't. Laughing to myself, I lay down on the couch and rested my eyes.

I woke up at 6pm and immediately started cooking. I threw the steaks in a pan and tossed a couple of potatoes in the oven to bake. I pulled out the broccoli vegetable mix to start it simmering. I put the candles on the dining room table and then finished setting it for dinner. After pulling a few of my flowers earlier, I put them in a vase, and sat it in the middle of the table. Everything was all coming along nicely.

Just as I got the potatoes out and the steaks on the plate, I heard Gabe arriving in my drive. Anticipating the knock and yelled, "Come on in!" Gabe entered, and I turned to greet him. He was wearing a long-sleeved black shirt with blue jeans, and ball cap on his head. He looked cute in a ball cap. I'd never seen him wear one before so I thought it was kind of odd, but cute nonetheless.

"Hi!" I said very cheerfully.

I walked up to him, but he turned the other way and said, "Hey." My hand reached for him, but only grazed the back of his shirt. He looked like he was alright, but he sure didn't act like himself.

"Are you alright, Gabe?" I asked him as I followed him to the table.

"Yeah, fine," he replied back. He looked at the table, and then sat in the chair closest to him. He would barely look at me, keeping his head down most of the time.

"It looks nice," he stated.

"Thank you. I hope you like steak and potatoes," I said back.

"Yeah, I don't know about those vegetables, but steak is good," he said as he scanned the table. "Got any beer?" Gabe's whole attitude was very odd; he seemed colder than usual. His expression was nothing close to a smile and his face seemed dull.

"Oh, no, I don't usually buy any, so I guess I didn't think about it. Sorry," I was beginning to think I made the wrong thing.

"I asked if I needed to bring anything. Why didn't you tell me to bring some?" he said rather hatefully.

"Well, if I knew you wanted it, then I would have. You could've just brought it if you wanted it so bad." I was starting to get irritated.

"Whatever," he said as he huffed. He reached across the table and grabbed the plate that was where I planned for him to sit. I sat across from him and watched for a minute. He picked up his silverware and started cutting up his steak. He broke open his potato and slathered butter all over it. "No sour cream?" he asked.

"I didn't think you liked sour cream, so no, I didn't pick any of that up either," I replied. I was starting to get angry instead of irritated. "Obviously I didn't do much right by the way you're acting."

Gabe looked up at me for a brief moment, and had surely seen that I wasn't happy. Without it appearing to bother him, he continued cutting up his steak. He took a few bites of his food and smarted off, "Not bad. Be better if you had beer to wash it down with though."

"Really? Well, if you want some beer so bad, Gabe, go buy it…and drink it alone at *your* house!" I said with my voice getting louder with each word. Gabe threw down his fork, and I jumped a little at the noise of it hitting his plate.

He stood up and angrily yelled, "Fine, I will get my own damn beer!"

He started walking to the door when I grabbed him by the arm and said, "What is your problem?"

"My problem? My problem is that you obviously don't know what I like! And don't touch me again, bitch!"

As he yelled he took a step closer to me and I backed up twice as far. He was really starting to scare me now, and I could feel my heart rate speed up in fear. Gabe never yelled at me like this, much less cussed and called me names. He stepped back and walked out the door, slamming it as he went. I hurried to the front door and watched him out the window. He even walked mad, taking long strides and throwing his arms in the air. He opened the door to his car, and got inside. I heard the engine start up, and I just stared at him. He stared back at me with such hate in his eyes. I saw a violet colored tint around his face and looked up at the yard light. I glanced back at him, as he had started to pull away. The tint was gone and I ignored it, thinking the light had reflected it onto his windshield. He fish-tailed his tires and drove right through my yard as he left.

"Really? Did he just drive through my nicely mowed yard? Did he actually just call me a bitch because I didn't have beer? What the hell?" I was talking to myself out loud. I walked back to the dinner table and stood there in utter disbelief of what had just happened. I was in shock and I was mad. I grabbed the dishes and glasses from the table and threw them in the sink. I tossed the food in the trash and said, "Hell with it!" as I walked away to my bedroom.

I paced, and paced, and paced some more. My mind wouldn't stop reeling over what had happened. I was angry and hurt over what he had said and done. He was like a different person. Where was the Gabe I made sweet, passionate love to in the woods the night before? Well, I will tell you where he wouldn't be, and that was by my side if he thought he was going to get away with this.

I changed into some pajamas and cuddled up in my bed. I thought really hard about texting Gabe and seeing just what his problem was, but I decided I really didn't even want to think of him anymore. I switched on the television to help empty my head, but as I tried and tried to not think about what happened, my eyes slowly filled with tears, and they streamed down my face.

CHAPTER 14

I didn't sleep worth a crap. When I awoke up my eyes were swollen shut and red. Clearly, I had been crying in my sleep; my eye lids were all puffed up and I had dark circles under them. "Great," I said out loud as I looked at myself in the bathroom mirror, "now I have to go to work looking like a freak!" I pulled out a washcloth and wet it down with cold water. I went back to my bed and lay on top of the covers, placing the cold cloth over my eyes. Hopefully, with a little bit of time, my eyes would relax and return to normal. However, my attitude still really sucked and I didn't see any way of quickly correcting that.

I was truly debating not going in today. I mean, Gabe could handle it and he made it clear I wasn't on his list of top priority people to see. After about twenty minutes of lying there, I walked into my bathroom to see if the damage had gotten any better. It hadn't. Maybe a little bit, but not enough to not look like I had a good batch of hives around my eyes. I decided I was going to skip work. I sent a simple text to Gabe:

Sick wont b n

I didn't think he deserved anything else. I wasn't feeling real good about not going in anyways, as it could give Gabe some sick satisfaction of ruining my day. I was still steaming mad at him for the previous night.

Are u alright? Do u need anything?

"Oh, now he's being all concerning, and wondering if I'm okay? Men!" I grumbled under my breath. I didn't even dignify that with a response.

I wandered into my kitchen and saw the mess from the previous night. I dumped the rest of the food, did the dishes, and cleaned up the table. I didn't have too much else to do, so I ran my hands under the cold water and splashed my face. I was feeling better; at least I could open my eyes all the way.

I drove into town to do a little grocery shopping and stopped by the diner. I saw Hank in the front booth talking to Joe. He was shimmering yellow and for the first time today, I smiled. A few new ghosts were wandering around the place, but nothing majorly bad. Joe hovered up to me and quietly asked, "Bekah, you okay? You don't look quite like yourself."

"I'm fine, Joe. Thank you for asking," I replied back.

"It's that no-good boyfriend, isn't it? Not good enough in the sack?" Walter said, on the other side of me.

"Walter!" I yelled out irritated.

"Oh, I'm sorry. Are you...unsatisfied?" he laughed, very amused with himself. I knew better than to let Walter get to me. He was completely harmless and loved to be a smart ass. Joe looked at me and just smiled, shaking his head side to side. I took a deep breath and thought before I answered, as I knew I was still in a crappy mood.

"Thank you for your concern, Walter," I stated as I turned to leave. I walked out to my SUV, and if my day couldn't get any better, there stood Gabe at my door.

"I thought you were sick, Bekah. What's up?" he asked, leaning in towards me for a kiss, but

I moved to the side. I opened my back door and pulled out a can of beer from my groceries.

"Here, now you have one for tonight…or would you rather the whole six pack? Would that make you happy?" I tossed the can of beer at him as hard as I could, it hitting him in the chest. I got in my car, started it up and drove away. All the while, Gabe stood there looking like an idiot.

Back home I put away the groceries and tossed the beer in my fridge. At twenty years of age, I was allowed to buy a certain amount of alcohol. There were all kinds of restrictions about what kind, but beer was one of the few things allowed. I lazily sat on the couch, and then I heard a car pulling in my drive. I got up to see Gabe exiting his car and then walking to my house. Great! I really didn't want to see him right now.

"Bekah?" He yelled as he knocked on the door. I stood up, but hesitated, wondering if I really wanted to talk to him or not. "Bekah…I know you're home. What's a matter with you?" he continued yelling through the door. I realized right then and there that I hadn't locked the door. If he really wanted to get in, he could. I quietly walked over to it. BANG, BANG. He slammed his fists on it, and I jumped at the unexpected noise. "Seriously...Why won't you talk to me? I can see you." I could hear his voice becoming more frustrated.

I gently locked the door and said back, "I don't want to see you now, Gabe. Just go home." My voice was starting to quiver and I told myself that I was absolutely not allowed to cry from sadness or anger.

"I'm sorry, Bekah, for whatever I did. Can't you at least talk to me?" his voice was getting quieter. I continued standing there.

"Just leave, Gabe," I said in a low hushed voice. "Just go."

I watched him turn to leave. He briefly stopped at the porch steps, and he looked to be debating if he should return or not. Instead, he walked out to his car and climbed in. He just sat there. What was he waiting for? I thought to myself. I wished he'd just leave already. After a few minutes, I heard the hum of his car, and he drove away. I relaxed my shoulders and went back to my couch. I was so confused. Was he was sorry for what he done? I was really starting to think that I simply wasnt cut out for girlfriend material, or maybe, and most likely, Gabe wasn't boyfriend material.

CHAPTER 15

I was standing in the middle of my room, all alone, wearing nothing but my shorts and tank top. It was empty of all furniture or items. The room seemed to be spinning and every time I tried to catch focus on something, the room would spin again. What the hell was going on? I started to feel dizzy and nauseous from the twirling. I suddenly caught a quick glance of Gabe standing in my bedroom corner. I saw him long enough to notice he had on his typical blue jeans and white t-shirt, but he disappeared as soon as I had seen him. Next, my parents showed up. Their lifeless bodies sat on a couch, shoved up against my bedroom wall; both with their blank, expressionless faces and the blood trickling down their faces.

"What's going on?" I screamed but they were gone before I got the words out of my mouth. Then, Uncle Cooper was sitting at the desk he always sat at. It was usually in the living room, but this time it appeared where my parents had been. His wire-rimmed glasses perched perfectly on his

nose, looking quite frustrated. He was screaming at me, but again, I couldn't hear anything.

The room spun a massively and multiple times when the images started over...Gabe stood, hunched over, in the corner, this time with blood all over him, dripping onto the floor. My parents sat lifelessly on the couch, but quickly fell off onto the floor with a thud. Then, Uncle Cooper ran towards me, his mouth screaming words but making no sound. All I could hear, though, was a loud, irritating buzzing noise, like a hive of bees was surrounding me. I shook my head, trying to stop the buzzing. I grabbed it with both my hands and screamed, "Stoooooppppppp!!!" but it did no good. The buzzing got louder, and just when I thought it would all be over, it started again.

My surroundings continued spinning, only to stop with each painful image. Gabe was now lying on the floor, pools of blood all around him and barely clinging to life. My parents were now completely on the floor, their bodies in mangled, unnatural positions. Then, when I was least expecting it, Uncle Cooper showed up right in front of my face... "DON'T TRUST HIM, BEKAH! HE'S

DANGEROUS!!! THINK!!!!!" Just as the buzzing disappeared, Uncle Cooper's voice echoed loudly, and I felt like my head was going to crack open. As quickly as he said it, he was gone, and I was left standing there, frantic breathing and my heart racing so fast I thought it was going to explode.

I awoke on the couch and could still feel my heart pumping harder than it ever had. I sat up, trying to think about the dream, and what the hell it all meant. My head ached and my stomach felt the residual nausea. I stood up, and walk to the front door. It had gotten dark outside. I peered through the window of my door, and saw the same 2 purple eyes peering back at me. I screamed and backed up. I was starting to think I was destined to have a heart attack today. I quickly grabbed my phone and dialed 911. I explained where I lived, and they assured me someone was on their way. I didn't have the guts to look back outside my front door as I couldn't get the image of those eyes out of my head and I didn't want to take the chance of seeing them again.

The pictures of Gabe, my parents, Uncle Cooper and the spine-chilling, angry, dark purple eyes haunted my vision. They reeled through my mind like a movie, repeating itself, and seemed never ending. I had to stop envisioning them. It was driving me crazy. I heard a knock at the door, and flinched. "We received a call. Are you okay?" I heard an older man's voice. I ran to the door, and chanced a look out. There stood Officer Lane at my door waiting for me.

I opened it and quickly told him to come in. "What the problem, Bekah? Damn, you're shaking like a leaf. Sit down, girl." He walked with me to the kitchen, and sat down at the table next to me.

I explained to him what had happened. "I know it sounds crazy, Henry, but please just check outside for me and make sure no one is out there. I won't be able to stay here unless I know everything is okay," I pleaded with him. Henry was an old friend of my Uncles, and had known me since I came to live in Jasper.

"No problem. I will check it out. You sit here, and try to calm yourself, ok?" Henry gave my hand a squeeze while he stood up. He walked out the door. I heard him on the radio with the department as he was calling for a few more officers to help him with the searching of my property.

I couldn't just sit there. I got up, and paced the floor in my living room. Walking back and forth I tore at my fingernails and cuticles. I saw more cars arriving at my house and Henry directing them where to go. The wait was agonizing. I knew in the back of my head though they wouldn't find anything. It would be stupid if the person was still hanging around outside.

After about an hour Henry came back inside and said, "Nothing, Bekah. Didn't see anyone or hear anything. However, did you know you had tire tracks in your yard?"

"Yeah, they're from the other day when my boyfriend and I got into a spat. He left rather irritated. Nothing major," I replied.

"Who's this boyfriend? I will make sure he had nothing to do with what happened tonight," Henry stated.

"Oh, no, I seriously doubt he was here tonight. He's wouldn't scare me like that, Henry," I tried to explain.

"Well, let's just make sure. Name?" He waited patiently.

"You know him, Gabe, my partner at the office. But I'm su-"

He interrupted me, "I know, I know, Bekah. Just let me make sure he's at home. At least let me do my job, okay?"

"Okay, if you say so, but I'm telling you he wouldn't do anything like this. Thanks for coming out, Henry," I said as he headed towards the door.

"No problem. Cooper would haunt my ass if I let anything happen to you on my watch, Bekah. I'll call you if anything comes up. Take care, and keep your doors locked. Call me if you need anything." Henry was a nice guy. He was in his 50's, tall with short, trimmed black hair. He had streaks of gray on the side that made him look more distinguished. He had been working at the police department for as long as I knew him.

I walked out on the porch with him as he left. I stood on the last step, and as I turned to go back to my door, something caught my eye. At the end of the steps closest to the underside of the porch was a beer can. Why was a beer can on my lawn next to my porch? I picked it up, and took it inside with me. It wasn't an old can. It was a new one and still had drops of beer inside it when I dumped it in my sink. I threw the can away in the trash. I had to calm myself, or I'd never get any sleep again. After locking all the doors and windows, I headed to my bedroom to try and relax.

CHAPTER 16

Tuesday morning came quickly as I awoke to my alarm sounding at 7am. It was gray and dreary outside looking to rain at any time. I got dressed and jumped in my car to head into work. I checked my phone and saw a text from Gabe.

Why did u send cops 2 my house last nite?

I knew I was going to have to face him at work so I might as well wait and just talk to him there. Honestly, I didn't have a clue what I was going to do about Gabe. I was still mad, or at least my feelings still were, and I really didn't feel like thinking about it.

Still not talkin 2 me?

Ugh, can't a girl get a break? I had approximately 15 minutes to figure out what the hell I was going to say, or do about him. I could stretch it out to about 45 minutes if I stopped at Del's for breakfast; maybe an hour if I stuck around and talked to Joe.

Guess not

I was now thinking of how I could start an argument with Walter, and that would take up even more time. I might as well just bite the bullet.

I pulled into work and walked in the office. Gabe was sitting at his desk talking to an elderly woman. I overheard her say her husband died and wanted Gabe to find him. Thank heavens he was busy. He looked up at me, we made brief eye contact, and I quickly looked away as I headed to my desk. No smile, no smirk, nothing. I kept my face as professional as I could.

I turned on my computer, and as I waiting for it to boot up I started the coffee maker. By this time, the woman had left. Gabe was standing against his desk, with his arms folded, staring at me. I could feel his eyes like laser beams boring into my head. "What?" I asked sharply not being particularly nice about it.

"What? What are you doing, Bekah? Is this your idea of pushing me away? Cause if it is you're doing a great job at it," he said as he continued to just stare at me.

"Push you away? I think you did a fine job of that all on your own, Gabe. Let's just work so this day can be over," I said back.

"No, not until you explain why the cops showed up at my house in the middle of the night checking to see where I was, or had been. What's going on?" I could tell Gabe was frustrated.

"I didn't send them to your house. Someone was at my house again last night, and I called the cops. They asked about the tire tracks in my yard. I told them it was from the other night, but they wanted to check on you to make sure. I never told them to go see you. If anything, I defended you. Stupid me!" I ranted.

"Ok, ok, can we take a few steps back here? I'm completely confused about what's going on. Why did you think someone was at your house? Why didn't you call me and why haven't you been talking to me? I went to your house and you sent me away. What the hell, Bekah? I thought we were dating, not ignoring each other," Gabe had walked over to the coffee pot and poured himself a cup. I went back to my desk and sat.

"Gabe, I had a really long night. My head hurts and the last thing I want to do is fight with you." I was rubbing the temples of my forehead with my fingers. I felt exhausted and I was so tired of thinking. "Can we just forget about the other night and move on? I'm willing, if you are," I asked him.

"I guess so. I mean, I don't even know-"

"--Okay, so it's forgotten then," I interrupted him. "What did that lady want? We need to track someone down?" I breathed in heavily and let the air out slowly as I tried to relax.

"Yes, I'm sure he will come around in the next couple days. I will keep my eye out for him." Gabe was sitting in his chair, just looking at me with an odd, puzzled look on his face.

The rest of the day went about the same way. It was pretty silent between Gabe and I, which was just fine with me. We had three people come in looking or asking about loved ones. My head pounded all day, and I really wanted to go home, and take a hot bath. "Wanna grab dinner with me?" Gabe asked.

"Um, not tonight Gabe. I just don't feel well," I responded half-heartedly.

"Ok, how about you come to my house? I will cook you dinner, rub your shoulders and you can just relax." Gabe smiled and his eyes lit up. I hated when he did that. It made saying no so much harder. However, this time it really wasn't that difficult.

"I promise you, Gabe, another time, ok? I'm just not in the mood. Rain check?" I asked him.

I could see the disappointment on his face as his smile vanished. "If that's the best I'm going to get, then I will take it," he answered.

I grabbed my stuff and headed to the door. "You lock up?" I asked him.

"Sure, if you will just come here for one minute," Gabe said as he stood up. I hesitantly walked over to him and stopped in front of his desk.

"I'm here. What do you need?" I asked him rather irritated.

"You. Will you stop being angry and look at me for one minute? That all I'm asking for," he pleaded.

"You got one minute," I said placidly and looked at my watch. Gabe walked around his desk and stopped. I tried to turn around, but he held my shoulders so I couldn't and started massaging them. It felt so good. I could feel all the tension release and my shoulders naturally dropped. I felt Gabe move my hair to one shoulder and lightly kiss my bare neck. I enjoyed it for about thirty seconds, but then I composed myself and stepped away from him. "Your minute is up. See you tomorrow," I said as I hustled out the door.

I told myself it was unacceptable to cry while I drove home. As my mind started to wander I realized how much I missed the feeling of his hands, the smoothness of his skin, and the warmth of his body. I missed his silly attitude and funny comments. I missed seeing him smile at me with his soft lips. However, it didn't take long until my mind wandered to the night he turned into an asshole and my once weak shell became hard again.

I got home about six pm and threw some soup on the stove. I wasn't really hungry, but I hadn't eaten all day so I knew I'd better have something. I poured it in a big mug, and walked to the front room.

Scanning the horizon out the front window, I noticed the gravel dust stirring on my drive. It was starting to get dark out, but it was still light enough to see. I saw Gabe's car driving down my lane. Why couldn't he just take no for an answer? Soon, he knocked on the door. I headed straight for it and said, "Gabe, I thought we agreed on a rain check?"

I opened it and Gabe said, "Well, I don't want you out here all alone, now do I?" He smiled. He was wearing another long-sleeved shirt and ball cap, reminding me of the disastrous night at my house a few days earlier.

I sighed. "Come in," I told him. I locked the door behind him, and sat on the couch.

"Got any beer?" He asked. My heart leaped. No, not again with the beer.

"Yeah, it's in the fridge," I hesitated at first, but replied back.

"Oh, good. You're a fast learner," he said. I started to think that if Gabe was going to be an ass again, then he should just leave. I still wasn't in a decent mood.

I heard the beer can open, and Gabe took a few swallows. "Since when did you start drinking so much beer?" I asked.

"Why does it matter to you?" he replied.

"It really doesn't, just something I noticed." Apparently he didn't like being questioned about his beer consuming either. I tried changing the conversation. "Did you find that woman's husband yet?" I thought maybe talking about work would be better.

"Why would I want to find someone's husband?" he replied as he took another swig.

"Why? I don't know, maybe because that's how you make money...so you can buy more beer." Maybe I was pushing it a little too much. Gabe tossed his can away and I heard him open the fridge and grab another one.

"Dammit, Bekah, get off my ass about the beer!" He yelled and swigged down another one. His demeanor wasn't even his own. He walked differently, talked differently; maybe he had a few beers before he even came over. Either way, I was not going to sit in my own house on pins and needles, not knowing if everything I said was right or wrong.

"I didn't ask you over here, Gabe. So if you are going to yell, or be an ass, then just leave now!" I yelled back. I saw Gabe from the corner of my eye walk from the kitchen to the living room. He stood next to me as I continued sipping on my soup.

To my surprise, my soup mug went flying across the room, and smashed into the wall, breaking the mug into pieces. I jumped up, glimpsed at Gabe, and then walked over to the broken pieces of mug on the floor. "What the hell, Gabe?" I yelled. All it took, though, was that one small glimpse to see that Gabe's beautiful, deep-ocean blue eyes had a flash of bone-chilling, deep purple color shoot across them.

I immediately took two steps back, as I suddenly knew I was in some serious trouble. With each step I took, Gabe advanced twice-fold on me. Soon, I was stuck with my back up against the wall. Gabe moved just close enough to me I could feel his breath when he spoke, "Damn, Bekah, why do we always have to fight? I just came over here for a little information." His creepy smile gave me goose bumps. His breath stunk of beer and nauseated me.

"You're not Gabe," I whispered.

"Well, whoo-hoo, the bitch finally got one right!" he yelled in my face. He grabbed a pair of gloves from his back pocket and put them on. He kept his eyes straight on me as he finished off his beer and threw the can thoughtlessly on the floor. He traced his gloved finger down my face and said, "I'm runnin' this show now, understand?"

I reached up to grab his face and he caught my arm mid-swing. "Uh, no, I don't think so. You won't be doing any touching tonight, Bekah, only me." His voice was rough and his face turned into a scowl as he lowered my arm to my side. I had to think and think fast. Hell, I had no idea what to do. I was starting to panic on the inside.

"I've been watching you for a while now, sweet thing. You do look good. I can see why Gabe likes you." He was starting to gross me out now.

"You want another beer?" I asked him quietly.

"Hell yeah, I do!" he replied. I stepped to the side of him and went into the kitchen, opened the fridge and grabbed a beer.

"Toss it to me!" he ordered. I threw the beer at him and went to sit back down on the couch.

"What do you want? Maybe I can help you," I asked him.

"Don't you try that ghostly bullcrap with me, Bekah! I won't have any of it, ya hear?" He was obviously getting more agitated, and he continued to drink down each beer in one swig. "We are doing this MY way, got that?" he continued.

"Yes, I got it," I replied in a quiet voice. Gabe continued pacing in the front room. I quickly considered on what to do. I hadn't ever dealt with this kind of ghost before, or at least I thought it was a ghost. I knew for damn sure it wasn't Gabe, not on the inside any ways. My stomach still felt sick and my head was throbbing. I felt like I was going to pass out.

"I need to lie down. I don't feel well," I said as I headed towards the couch.

"Oh, no, you get up. You get up and don't move!" He yelled.

Damn, did he think I had a hearing problem too, because he definitely yelled a lot. I stopped and stood at the end of the couch.

"You look so much like her," he said in his raspy voice as he stared at me. "Take off your shirt."

"Excuse me?" I asked.

"You heard me, Miss Priss. GET. UNDRESSED!" He was straight up in my face. I knew this was probably going to be my only chance at this, so I reached up with the opposite hand and grabbed Gabe's throat, hoping in my mind that I didn't do anything that would harm Gabe himself.

My mind immediately spiraled, racing on where to go, or what to do. I really didn't care about the ghost's past at the moment. I just needed to get him out of Gabe's body. Images flashed in my head; a little boy getting beat with bat, a man yelling obscene things, a woman being raped...all the while I was shifting through the ghosts mind to find something that I could grab onto. I really had no idea what I was supposed to do. Cooper never told me that this was even possible, much less how to do it. I, then, saw a pair of evil purple eyes glowing. "You're leaving!" I yelled to the ghost.

"Oh, I don't think so, bitch, and neither are you." He had a maniacal, crazy laugh. He couldn't keep me in here with him, could he?

I quickly reached out to touch the glowing eyes, not knowing if it would do any good or not but I felt my fingers grasp them. "Get out. Get out! GET OUT!" I screamed as loud as I could in his head. I hadn't ever entered a living person's mind so I quickly assumed I was in the ghosts head. As I yelled with all my conviction, I yanked the purple eyes as hard as I could and flew myself out of the ghosts mind taking the purple haze with me. One image flashed past me as I had let go of the ghost, an image I would never forget. It was an image of my mother and father sitting on their couch with a bullet hole in each of their heads.

I was back in my own mind now and the dizziness was far worse when compared to any previous times. I was dry heaving and shaking all over. The room was spinning and twirling out of control. Gabe's limp body collapsed to the floor with a loud thud. I saw the purple-aura ghost standing next to me. "See you next time," he whispered in my ear and swooshed away into the air.

CHAPTER 17

I sat on the floor trying to get my mind straight. The spinning in my head continued and I felt like I was going to puke non-stop. I tried holding in the heaves, luckily nothing came up with them. I kept trying to get to Gabe. Every movement I made towards him seemed like it pushed him further away. I could see him and he was breathing, but there were multiples of him due to the dizziness. I decided to stop for a minute. I laid back, closed my eyes, and took deep inhales to try and calm myself. I could feel my hands shaking and I had trouble controlling my breathing. I continued taking long, slow ragged breaths to help myself relax.

After several minutes I started to feel better. I wasn't as shaky and the dizziness, although not completely gone, was much better. I was dry heaving anymore so that was a plus. I slowly sat up to a sitting position and remained there for a few more minutes as I allowed myself to re-orient. I started moving towards Gabe, little by little. "Gabe!" I called out to him. No response.

"Gabe!" I yelled a little bit louder. Still, no response. I was close enough now to touch his hair. I ran my fingers through it and continued saying his name. I made it to the front of his body and grabbed his face with both my hands. "Gabe, you have to wake up!" I had tears forming in my eyes as the horrible thoughts of him never waking entered my mind. "Dammit, Gabe. Wake up!" I yelled at him, as I grabbed his shoulders shaking him.

The tears were flowing down my cheeks as I sat hopelessly beside him. I had no idea what to do, or how Gabe had been affected. I couldn't move him by myself especially since I was so weak. I stood up, slowly and steady, then carefully walked to my room. I grabbed a blanket and pillow and using the wall to help keep me from falling, I made my way back to Gabe. I placed the pillow under his head, covered him with the blanket and laid down right beside him. I could hear the beating of his heart as I put my head on his chest. Between that, and the steady rising of his chest, I constantly reminded myself Gabe was alive. I closed my eyes and allowed the exhaustion to overcome me as I fell asleep.

I awoke several hours later with my head still on Gabe's chest. I felt much better as all the dizziness was gone. My stomach felt normal and my head no longer throbbed. I immediately touched Gabe's face with my hand and quietly said, "Gabe, you have to wake up now." Gabe moved his head slightly and I knew he heard me. "Gabe, please, open your eyes and wake up," I said a little bit louder. Gabe rolled his head towards me and opened his eyes. I couldn't have been happier when I saw those blue eyes staring back at me.

"Are you alright?" I asked him.

"Yeah, I think so," Gabe sat up and looked around the room. "Bekah, why am I on your floor?" He asked beginning to realize where he was. "...with a pillow and blanket?" He continued. "What is going on?" He was clearly confused, and seemed to not remember what had happened.

"Gabe, are you ok? How do you feel?" I asked him.

"Well, I'd be a lot better if I knew what was going on. I feel like I have a hangover. Did we drink, Bekah?" He asked.

"What's the last thing you remember?" I asked him.

"Well, I asked you to dinner, you said no and gave me a rain check," he said rolling his eyes. "I locked up the office and went home. I started making some dinner..." Gabe's voice trailed off. He picked his hand up to his forehead and rubbed it a little. "What's happening, Bekah? Why can't I remember how I got on the floor of your front room? How did I even get to your house? Everything just kind of goes blank." Gabe stared at me with his eyes begging for an explanation.

"Come sit on the couch and I will explain what I know. Are you hungry? You did drink a lot of beer last night," I asked him.

"Beer? Bekah, I only drink an occasional beer. You know that," he replied back.

"Yes, normally you do, but not when you are possessed by a really pissed off ghost, Gabe," I said, and began explaining what had happened.

Over the course of an hour I detailed out what had happened. I cooked us both some scrambled eggs and toast; although, for now Gabe settled for coffee. I went further back and told him about the dinner at my house. Gabe didn't interrupt or question too much. He just let me talk. After I was all done, Gabe said, "Well, at least now I understand why you wouldn't speak to me. I called you a bitch, drank lots of beer and was generally a total ass to you."

I laughed out loud, "Well, yes, but I was more worried about you being a real jackass or, I don't know, being possessed by a purple ghost? What the hell are we going to do about that, Gabe?" I ate my breakfast and smirked at him. "Have you ever dealt with one of those ghosts before? Honestly, I'm a little freaked out! I didn't know if I could get him out of you!" My voice was getting ragged as I just stared at Gabe with feelings of hopelessness. "I've never yanked a ghost out of a person before, Gabe. I had no idea what I was doing. It scared the hell out of me," I said with my eyes glistening.

"But you did. You did get him out, Bekah." Gabe crossed over and hugged me. "I'm sorry. I'm so sorry for the way I behaved and what I put you through."

I kept my arms around him, part of my mind relieved he was possessed and truly not a bad guy. "Don't apologize, Gabe. It wasn't your fault. I should've noticed something sooner. I knew you weren't acting right, but I was starting to think a relationship brought the bad out in you. Honestly, I'm glad I was wrong." I let go of him and stepped back.

"I'm wondering why? Why did he choose me? Why did he choose you to harass? There's got to be a connection, Bekah," Gabe said as he sat back down and started picking at his food.

I took the dishes to the sink, ran some water and stood there as it started to fill. Those were all very good questions and I have no idea how to answer them. I knew very little about this actually. I read very little of him and I seriously doubted it would be easy to read him again. Cooperative isn't a word I would use to describe this ghost. "Bekah?" Gabe said, and pulled me out of my string of thoughts. "Turn the water off and come here. Come sit and we will figure this out." Gabe moved to the couch and patted the cushion next to him.

"What do we know about all this?" Gabe started. "I know that when being possessed I black out and have no memory of the events. I know that when he came out, or you yanked him out of my mind, I slept for hours. I still don't feel like myself entirely. It's like a residual feeling after you've been sick. Achiness, tired…ya know what I mean, Bekah? I could sleep for another day," Gabe said as he grabbed my hand.

"Well, I know," I said, "that he's not easy to get out of your head. He is unusually strong and very angry, almost crazy angry. I didn't have time to read him, but I did see small pieces. I know that your eyes got flashes of purple in them when he possessed you." I stopped and rubbed my temples.

"You're head hurt?" Gabe asked.

"Yeah, but only enough to bug me," I responded. Gabe sat side ways on the couch and motioned for me to turn around.

"What do you remember seeing, Bekah? Try to remember the details." I turned around and felt Gabe start massaging my shoulders.

"I saw a little boy being hit by a bat. He couldn't have been more than six or seven years old. It was horrible. He was hurt, crying and lying on the ground. Then, I saw a man yelling cruel, hurtful things to someone. I'm not sure who, I only saw him, the ghost, when he was alive, yelling. Afterward, I saw a woman being raped, I think she was anyways. I didn't see her face. I only saw the man ripping her clothes off and cursing at her." I stopped for a minute to catch my breath. "And lastly, I saw my parents, Gabe. I saw them sitting on the couch with...How did he have memories of my parents?" I took a deep breath and relaxed my shoulders. So many images were running through my brain and questions I didn't have any answers for. I wasn't sure if I would ever have the answers.

Gabe asked, "Did you recognize him at all? Anything about him seem familiar to you?"

"No, not at all. I have no idea who he is. I've never seen him before. I know that when I grabbed him, and yanked him out with me, I was sick. I felt sicker than ever before when I entered a ghosts mind. It was horrifying and it took all I had to get out. I wasn't sure if I'd even get out," I tried explaining. "Did Uncle Cooper ever tell you anything about these ghosts? He trained you," I asked.

"No, just that they were dangerous. He trained you too, Bekah. He rarely spoke of them to me," he stated.

"Right. He never said anything to me about them either…not then, anyways," my voice trailed off.

CHAPTER 18

We both decided it would be best to go and talk with Joe at the diner. I was hoping he would be able to offer some information on these ghosts. We drove into town and found Joe sitting in his usual spot. "Joe, do you mind if we talk for a bit?" I asked him. Both Gabe and I sat down in the booth across from him after he shook his head.

"What's up, Bekah?" Joe asked in a serious manner.

"Can you possess a living being, Joe?" I asked him.

Joe looked at me with a bit of shock and replied, "No, I cannot. Why are you asking?"

I explained to Joe what had happened with Gabe. Joe listened intently and when I was done talking, he said, "Well, anger can drive anyone to do crazy, unusual things so I don't doubt a ghost that angry could accomplish that. I don't see many of those types of ghosts around, and when I do I tend to keep my distance." Joe sat at the table; his arms folded in front of him and gave a concerned smile. "You seem to be in a bit of trouble. Do you know this guy from anywhere?"

I thought about that question again and said, "No, I don't. Gabe asked me the same thing, but I have no idea who he is. Have you seen him around, Joe?" I asked with curiosity.

"Nope. Sure haven't," he replied.

Walter walked by us. He stopped in front of our booth and stood there quietly not stating one smartass word. That was very odd for Walter. "Hello, Walter," I said. He continued to stand there. He didn't say anything back, just folded his arms and yawned. I turned my attention back to Joe. "Thank you, Joe. If you see him around then let me know, will you?"

Joe smiled and said, "You got it."

I started to scoot out of the booth when Walter said, "Well, what am I, invisible? I'm not that damn lucky, to be an invisible ghost you can't see. Why don't you ask me anything?" I looked at Gabe and shrugged my shoulders.

Gabe replied, "Have you seen a purple-aura ghost roaming around Del's?"

"Not you, dumbass! I meant Bekah! Oh, forget it." He grumbled and walked away.

I immediately got out of the booth and headed towards him. "Walter, have you seen one roaming around? Please, talk to me. It's important," I pleaded with him.

"Actually, yes, I have. He's one mad, crazy son of a bitch and he wants you." He pointed to me as he said it. "I've heard him ranting on some occasions. I don't know how he knows you, but he does. He says you look 'too much like her' and he "has to know'."

"Like who?" I asked Walter.

"Well, how the hell am I supposed to know? I can't read his mind. That's your job, isn't it? It's just what he repeats all the time. He isn't here often, but when he is, he says the same thing over and over. He has been roaming for a long time." Walter turned to walk away.

"Wait!" I called out to him. "Do you know of any way we can keep him from possessing people?"

"Nope," Walter said as he continued to walk away. "You're on your own, Princess." Then, he disappeared into the air.

"Great," I said aloud to myself. "Thanks, Walter," I spoke just in case he was still around. I turned to Gabe. "Let's head home. I think for now we should stick together. That way we can keep an eye on each other in case he decides to show back up. Are you good with that, Gabe?" I asked.

Gabe took a deep breath and sighed. "Well, I guess I'll deal with it." He smiled at me and held out his hand. We walked out to the car to drive back to my house.

We stopped by Gabe's to pick up some clothes and necessities for him. He packed a bag for himself and I wandered into his kitchen. "Anything you want from in here?" I hollered to him. As I did, I opened the fridge. Damn, the whole thing was filled with beer! Gabe walked into the room and noticed it as well.

"No, but hell, I must've hit up every store there was. Don't bring any of it, Bekah," he said.

"Good, I was hoping you would say that. Apparently this ghost likes beer, or at least did like it." I watched Gabe finish packing and walked to the door.

"That would be fine if it wasn't me that dealt with the after effects of it," Gabe added.

We made it to my house and had a quiet dinner. It was nice being around Gabe when he was his usual self. I couldn't believe I allowed myself to think so negatively about him. I should've seen he was different for a reason. I felt rather guilty for calling him an ass when it wasn't even his fault. Afterwards, I took a shower and relaxed in my comfy pajamas. Gabe was watching television in the front room. "Gabe," I called to him, "would you mind sleeping next to me tonight?"

Gabe turned and gave me a smile, then reached down and turned off the set. "You don't have to ask Bekah." He walked towards me.

"Thanks," I said as I walked to my bed. "I've been having nightmares lately and don't want to sleep alone."

"You don't have to make excuses to sleep with me," Gabe replied with a laugh, "I can't keep the nightmares away, but I will be here if you wake up from one." He climbed in the bed next to me. I breathed a little bit easier when I felt his arms cradle me. He softly kissed my neck and we both fell asleep.

CHAPTER 19

I am in a pitch black room with one small light shining down on me. I can barely see past my outstretched hand. I slowly walked around the room to figure out where I was, but there's no walls, no objects in the room and the floor is made of dirt. I continue to search, all the while the small light above me stays shining down. "Hello?" I called out. No response from anything. How does this light keep following me? Suddenly, I hear the buzzing noise. Not again, I really didn't want to have the bees surrounding my mind again. The further I walked, the louder it became. I stopped and stood in the dark room in hopes that the buzzing would end, too. "Hey!" I yelled out. Complete quietness all around me.

I sat on the dirt for a little bit and drew figures with my fingers. How long was I going to just sit here? Soon, the buzzing noise disappeared and faint footsteps replaced the sound. I could hear each step, slowly walking, becoming louder and louder. I quickly stood up and started walking again. The footsteps picked up in pace and it made my heart quicken. They sounded heavy, like someone in a pair of boots. My anxiety was quickly escalating and I began to panic. I started turning where I stood, trying to see who was approaching me. I couldn't tell which direction the footsteps were coming from. I turned again to look behind me and suddenly right in front of me stood Uncle Cooper. "We don't have much time, Bekah. You are in danger," he stated.

"I know, but I don't know what to do to stop it, Uncle Coop. Tell me what to do," I pleaded.

"There are things you don't know, events you aren't aware of yet. I don't have time to go into those things now," Cooper said with a sense of urgency. I heard the buzzing start up again.

"What is that?" I asked.

"Focus, Bekah. Listen to me!" His voice getting louder, but at the same time was getting drowned out by the buzzing. "Lo.. ... th... ..sk!" He was struggling to talk loud enough.

"I can't hear you, Coop!" I yelled back. All I could hear was pieces of what he was saying while the buzzing took over my ears.

"DESK!" He yelled at me as loud as he could. I jumped from how his voice echoed through the dark room and then, he was gone. The loud buzzing continued. My head was starting to ache and that horrible feeling of dizziness was starting to take control again.

"Bekah" I heard someone call for me. The voice seemed so far away. "Bekah!" I heard again. That was Gabe's voice.

"Gabe?" I yelled back. The buzzing was so loud now that I couldn't even hear myself speak. I had no choice but to sit back down, that or I was going to fall down. Quickly thereafter, the dizziness that waved through my head took over and blackness fell over me.

"Bekah, wake up!" I heard Gabe say. I quickly sat up in bed and took a sharp breath in.

"Gabe, what's wrong?" I asked.

"Nothing is wrong with me, Bekah. It's you. You were yelling for your Uncle and had your hands over your ears. What's wrong? Did you have another nightmare?" He asked as he climbed out of bed and wetted a washcloth with cold water. He brought it over and put it on my forehead.

"Yeah, bad dream, but I don't think it was meant to be. We have to go through my uncle's desk, Gabe." I got out of bed and headed to the front room.

"Now? It's like 3am, Bekah," Gabe questioned.

"Yes. Now, Gabe. We have to find something," I tried to explain. I started throwing open the drawers and searching through papers. I never really went through the desk after Cooper died.

"What are we looking for?" Gabe asked.

"I don't know. I just know we have to go through this desk. Please don't think I'm crazy, but my Uncle told me to get in his desk. I have no idea why, but I'm trying to figure it out. Will you help me?" I said to Gabe. I continued dumping the drawers out on the floor.

"Of course I will," he answered and immediately started looking through the papers.

We both pulled out all the drawers of the desk and searched through Uncle Cooper's things. We found some old tax files, lots of receipts and bank statements. We found piles of paper clips, staples, pens and blank paper, but nothing that really meant anything to either of us. "I don't know, Gabe. This isn't getting us anywhere," I said out of frustration. I sat on the floor with piles of papers surrounding me. "We looked in every drawer. There's nothing that will help us with that crazy ghost. I don't understand." I put my head in my hands and tried hard to remember everything in my dream.

"Has this desk always been here, Bekah?" Gabe questioned as he looked around the room.

"Yeah, I didn't move anything after Coop died. Everything is the same as it was," I explained. The desk was up against the corner in the living room wall. It was an old desk with three drawers on the right side, one long drawer in the middle and two on the left side. It was a dark cherry red wood with a few circular coffee stains from where my Uncle constantly sat his coffee cup.

Gabe got up and walked into the kitchen, "Where do you keep your tools at, Bekah?" He asked.

"My tools? What for?" I asked back, and was getting a little worried about what he wanted to do. I kept them in a drawer next to my silverware in the kitchen. Just as I was about to answer him, Gabe found them. He grabbed a hammer and flat screwdriver and then returned to the desk.

"We are going to take it apart. Ready?" He looked at me with all seriousness and handed me the hammer.

"No, we can't take it apart. It belonged to my Uncle. I don't want it broken," I exclaimed back.

"We won't break it, but obviously your Uncle has something he wants you to find in this desk. So, we need to find it," he said as he started to examine the desk. Gabe grabbed a hold of the desk and pulled it out from the corner of the wall. I shoved away all the stuff on the floor to make room. As Gabe walked behind the desk, he said, "Never mind. I think I just found something." He bent down behind it.

"Found what, Gabe?" I asked and jumped up. He walked out from behind the desk and handed me a book. It was a thick, brown, leather book held closed with a white shoelace. "Couldn't he find something besides a shoelace to tie it with?" I laughed. "You are awesome, Gabe! Thank you! Let's see what it says," I told him and sat on the couch.

Gabe sat next to me as I untied the lace and started looking through it. "Seems like he kept a journal of all the ghosts he came across," I explained to Gabe. Page after page the journal held stories of different ghosts my Uncle Cooper had seen, or helped. The journal dated back to before I was born. "I'm going to read for a while, Gabe," I told him as I headed back to my warm bed. I climbed in and started at the beginning.

Gabe climbed in next to me and said, "Let me know if you find anything interesting. I'm going to...watch some cartoons," He said as he leaned in and kissed my lips.

CHAPTER 20

As I read my uncle's journal I felt I was invading his privacy. It held not only notes about ghosts he came across, but also personal feelings about people he met and knew, including my parents.

1994: Got in a huge fight with Sam. He's never liked the idea that I can talk to ghosts. Not like I asked for the damn ability. He doesn't want me around Bekah. When I brought up the idea that she may be able to talk to them too, he completely flipped. He told me to stay away from him and his family. Bekah is my only niece and I can't even see her. Dammit!! No way of knowing now if she can communicate with ghosts, or even read them. I doubt I will ever know.

I would've been two years old then, I thought to myself. No wonder I didn't know who he was when he came and picked me up at the police station. My dad wouldn't allow him to see me. I felt kind of bad for my Uncle. He was a good man and raised me well. I continued reading another story.

1995: A woman came to see me today. She lost her husband. She asked me to try and find him so she could be sure he was okay. I found him wandering around Del's. He had a blue aura when I talked to him the first time. He was sad he left his wife behind. I offered to read his mind and see if I could help him. He agreed to it. I read he had a wonderful life with his wife and children. He was sad, but I helped him find peace. He died of a massive heart attack. His name is Joe.

"Hey, Gabe, this has Joe in it. My uncle helped him," I said. However, Gabe wasn't listening because he fell asleep watching the cartoons. I found I had been skipping around in the book. I went to the year my parents died.

1999: Got a call from the police. Sam and Abby were found shot in the head. What in the hell happened to them? I can't believe my brother is dead. I now have my niece, Bekah. She is the only family I have left. I will do my best to raise her. She's as beautiful as her mother was, but she has my eyes. I wonder if she will be able to communicate with ghosts. I will do as my brother wanted and not tell her anything about it. Maybe her life will be easier if she doesn't even know people like me exist. I will wait and see.

Well, I obviously took after my Uncle. He really didn't have any choice but to tell me after I seen my first ghost. My eyes were getting heavy and I could feel the tears forming in them when I read about my parents. My uncle didn't even know what happened. At least not yet he didn't. I wondered if he ever figured out who shot them and why. I'm pretty sure he would've told me if he had known, but thinking back I never specifically asked him what he knew. My mind was fascinated and exhausted by this journal all at the same time. It held so many stories, and I knew I couldn't read it in one night, much less a few hours. I lied down next to Gabe and rested my head on his shoulder. I made a mental note that I needed to search for dark-purple aura ghosts. I closed the book and stuffed it underneath my pillow.

I awoke a few hours later and heard Gabe gathering things in the front room. I saw him grab the car keys. "Where are you going?" I asked concerned.

"I have to run into the diner, Bek. I have to see if that lady's husband has come in yet. I will be back soon." He turned and looked at me. "Don't worry; I wasn't going to leave without telling you. I left a note for you; however, I think my note is much better than the one you left for me." He grinned and came to kiss me. "Honestly, I was hoping you wouldn't even wake up until I came back. I wasn't planning on being gone long."

"Do you think that is a good idea, though? What if that ghost finds you again?" I questioned.

"Bekah, if he is going to find me, then he will find me no matter where I am. At this point I can't stop him from doing anything," Gabe stated.

"Yes, that's true, but I was hoping he wouldn't be as prone to hopping inside your head if we stayed together. I barely got him out of you once, I don't know if I can do it again, Gabe," I tried pleading my argument.

"I think you can do more than you give yourself credit for, Bekah. I promise I will be back soon, within the hour. If I need more time I will call you. Don't worry. Read your Uncle's journal and see if you can learn anything else. I will see you soon." Gabe ran his finger down my cheek and kissed me gently. He reached down and squeezed my hand, then turned and walked out the door.

I started cleaning up the mess in the front room from the desk drawers. I filed everything as it was and arranged the desk neatly. I pushed it back into the corner where it belonged and grabbed the journal from under my pillows. Snatching my cell phone from the dresser, I silently hoped nothing bad would happen to Gabe.

CHAPTER 21

2005: January-Bekah's 13th birthday this month. I took her to Del's for dinner and she seen her first ghost. She seemed a little frightened so I really felt no choice but to help her understand why she was seeing them. I knew my brother didn't want her having anything to do with ghosts, but if she ignores them they will just keep bothering her. I taught her about the sad ghosts and she did amazingly well for her first time. It was helpful the ghost was just a child and was just as scared herself. Bekah definitely inherited my abilities.

I was feeling quiet thankful Cooper was around to help me learn and understand what was happening. If I had seen the ghosts and my dad was around I probably would've grown up in a looney bin, I chuckled to myself. I read a few more stories as I thumbed through the book. He made so many entries about the ghosts he came across. I was thinking I wouldn't ever come across one about a purple aura ghost. Maybe Cooper hadn't seen one either. That didn't make a lot of sense in my head though, seeming how Cooper was the one telling me to read his journal. I got up and made myself a cup of tea and continued scanning the book. I don't know how long I had been sitting on the couch reading when Gabe returned. "Any luck with finding the lady's husband?" I asked him.

Gabe replied, "Nope, nothing new at the diner. How's the journal reading going?"

I shrugged my shoulders and huffed. "Nothing major so far." I approached Gabe and stared into his eyes. I just wanted to make sure he was actually Gabe. I touched his arm, felt the small sparks and knew he was all right.

"I'm me, Bekah. No worries," Gabe laughed. I returned to the couch feeling relieved nothing had happened.

"I just had to make sure." I said, feeling a little bit foolish. I picked up the journal and continued to flip through it. One page caught my eyes as the corner had been flipped down.

1998: September 28- I came across my first dark purple aura ghost today. He was a mean creature. I saw him from a distance. I yelled out to him, but he just screamed at me to leave him alone. He was wandering through town and as he walked away I saw him look back at me. I think I can help him. Just have to get him to understand that. I could see the fury rolling off him. He was quite a sight to look at. He looked vaguely familiar. Definitely gave me a feeling of fear by just looking at him. Wish I could get a closer look at him.

September 29-Saw him again, this time as I was walking through the woods. I yelled at him to stop and talk to me. He just kept walking. I ran to catch up with him, but he disappeared. I quickly drove back into town and went to Del's hoping find him there, but he wasn't. Why is he roaming around Jasper? What does he want? I intend to find out.

"I found something, Gabe!" I yelled out even though he was right beside me.

October 12—Mean ghost, very mean and dangerous ghost. I only wanted to help him, but he is far beyond help. I saw him at the library and decided to just jump in and read what he was thinking. Maybe get some insight. That didn't go well. He has a lot of blocks up in his head. I could barely see how he died, but I realized I knew him. He is filled with such hatred for everything. When I left him I was terribly sick. He knocked a shelf of books on me and said if I ever did that again he would kill me. I told him I could help him. He yelled saying he didn't want any help. And then, I watched him step in to a living person. I'd never seen anything like it. He just stepped right into a young lady. That lady walked up to me as I lie on the floor with books all over me. She raised her leg up and brought her high heel down on my neck. She held her foot there and told me if I ever seen him again to just walk the

*other way because I wouldn't live. After she
released me, I asked him how he possessed
other people. He didn't answer, removed
himself from the woman and walked away.
The unknowingly woman collapsed to the
floor. This isn't good. The ghost is Bobby.*

"Well, at least we know everyone passes out after being possessed. It's not just you. And we have a name," I said to Gabe.

He chuckled and responded, "Great." I could tell Gabe was getting restless. He hated sitting around doing nothing.

I put the journal down and asked, "Do you want to do something, Gabe? You seem a little anxious."

Gabe tossed the remote on the coffee table, stood up and stretched. "Honestly, Bekah, I think I'll go out for a run. I feel cooped up and I just need to burn some energy," Gabe replied.

I stood up next to him and said, "Ok, well, go run then. I'll be here if you need anything. Take your phone with ya, ok?"

Gabe grabbed his phone, walked around the table and stopped. He leaned in and kissed me. I felt his arms wrap around my waist and he placed his forehead to mine. "I will only be gone for about an hour. You see or hear anything odd, call me immediately. I'll just run your drive or through the woods, ok?" He pulled himself away and walked towards the door.

I mentioned back, "Be careful. See you soon." Gabe walked out the door and started running up the drive.

I could understand how Gabe was feeling. I was also tired of just sitting around, but I really wanted to find out all I could about this ghost. I picked back up the journal and began where I left off.

I read page after page of the journal. Uncle Cooper seen the ghost multiple times afterward, but because he didn't know how to deal with him, he did as the ghost said and kept his distance. Cooper was very frustrated with this though, because he knew he was dangerous and didn't really want him wandering around hurting people.

"Ugh, Coop, what am I supposed to be reading here? You aren't giving me anymore info than I already have," I said out loud to myself. I put the journal down. I couldn't read anymore. I needed a break. I looked up at the clock and seen it was four pm. How long had Gabe been gone? What time did he leave? I was concentrating so hard on the journal I hadn't paid any attention to the time.

I grabbed my phone and sent a text to Gabe.

How's the run?

He didn't respond, but it really didn't surprise me considering he was probably listening to music as he ran. I got up and looked out the front room window. I saw Gabe walking down the drive. I stepped out on to the front porch and sat on the top stair waiting for him. He suddenly stopped. I stared at him and wondered what he was doing. I scanned the area trying to understand why he was just standing in the middle of the gravel drive, but couldn't see anything around him. I could even make out Gabe moving his lips, like he was talking to someone. I got up and started heading up the drive towards him.

The closer I got to him, the quicker my pace became. I suddenly realized Gabe was standing in the middle of the drive talking to the purple-aura ghost. Not good. Gabe looked up and seen me coming towards him, as did the ghost. "Stop, Bekah!" yelled Gabe. Is he nuts? I wasn't about to just stand there and watch him get possessed. I continued towards him, getting closer. I can see they were still talking, but I couldn't make out any words. "Bekah! Trust me! Stay back!" Gabe ordered me and he put his hand out to make a stopping motion. I did trust Gabe so without really thinking too much about it, I stopped walking. I could hear scattered and whispered words between them, but nothing that made any sense.

I watched intently, staring hard at the ghost and praying that Gabe knew what the hell he was doing. I continued watching for a few minutes and then I heard Gabe yell, "No, you said you wouldn't!" Gabe took two steps back away from the ghost and I took off running towards them again. "Bekah, I'm going to need that help now!"

Gabe hollered towards me as he continued to back away from the ghost.

"Block him out, Gabe!" I screamed to him. However, as I got close enough to reach out and grab Gabe, the ghost walked right into him, disappearing into Gabe's body and mind.

Well, this was just freaking great, I thought to myself. So much for "Trust me". I quit running and stopped directly in front of the now possessed Gabe.

"Hello, again Bekah. I told you we'd see each other again." Gabe's face turned towards me with an evil smile. His dimples didn't even look cute now. His voice was lower and more gruff than usual.

"Damn! What do you want?" I asked him angrily and filled with fear. I knew I could probably get a hand on him since Gabe was wearing only shorts and a t-shirt.

"Don't even think about it, Bekah. Move ahead of me and we will talk as we head back to your house." I took a few steps ahead of him and started walking.

"What are we talking about exactly? I don't have much to say to you unless you are going to tell me your name and why you are causing so much trouble," I informed him. He wouldn't respond. He kept quiet as we reached the porch and continued inside my house.

"My name is not important for you to know yet. Now...undress!" He ordered. He continued to stand along the opposite side of the living room.

"NO, and I'm beginning to think you are a pervert!" I yelled back. Gabe's face turned a shade of red and he headed to the kitchen. I saw purple flash across his eyes.

He grabbed a steak knife, immediately held it to his wrist and said, "I really don't think you realize what exactly I am capable of. Maybe I need to show you." He quickly ran the knife across his wrist and blood spurted out everywhere. I took a quick, deep breath in and started to yell, but he spoke first. "I don't feel a thing, Bekah. Now, are you going to cooperate or do I need to give more examples?" A disgusting, satisfying grin formed across his face. I was starting to think I had no choice but to comply. I certainly didn't want Gabe to get hurt. I knew I wasn't going to get close enough to get a hand on him.

"Fine, but you are going to answer a few questions if you expect me to follow your orders," I said as I took off my shoes. "Your name?" I asked him. I needed to be sure this was the same ghost my Uncle had dealt with.

He just laughed and shook his head. "Just like your Uncle. He thought he could control me too, but he quickly realized he couldn't. As will you, but I will humor you for a bit...Bobby. Take off your shirt."

I reached down, pulled my shirt up over my head and tossed it on the floor beside me. "Happy?" I said sarcastically.

"Not yet...now pants," he again ordered. I was quite surprised that I wasn't freaking out more than I was. However, it helped to keep in my head that Bobby couldn't really do anything to me. After all, if he got close enough to touch me, then that meant I could touch him and he definitely didn't want that. I took off my pants and stood in the living room in just my black bra and panties.

I tossed my arms up and sarcastically asked, "Now what...*Bobby*?"

Bobby started to circle the room, keeping his eyes on me. I could feel him staring and I was starting to feel a little humiliation mix in with my anger. "Turn around," he once again ordered.

"Have you ever heard of the word please?" I shot back at him. I quickly regretted my choice of words as he slashed Gabe's other wrist. My humiliation was quickly drowned out by my anger. I could feel my face getting warm and flush red. I decided I was done playing this little game. I didn't turn around, but instead ran right for him. He was going to hurt Gabe regardless so I saw no further reason to cooperate. I threw my arm out to grab him and Gabe's body quickly fell to the floor. Bobby was standing a few feet from him with his purple aura violently gushing around him. I grabbed towels and wrapped Gabe's wrists to help stop the bleeding.

"I need one more thing, Bekah. Shall I return at a later date or can we wrap things up now?" He asked with an evil sneer.

I responded with hatred, "Other than me kicking your ass, I won't be doing anything else. I don't care what you need!" Bobby quickly moved and was now standing directly in front of me.

"Give me Cooper's book and I will be on my way!" he shouted.

I looked straight into his evil, dark purple eyes and said, "I will be on my way into your head if you don't back the hell up!" This sent him reeling with laughter. A hoarse, rough laughter that sent chills up my body.

"You think I would get this close if you could cause harm to me? You can't hurt me, Bekah! Your Uncle couldn't hurt me and neither can you!" He roared his words at me. Bobby then stepped a few feet back. Right before he disappeared he smiled and said, "Guess we will have a later date then."

CHAPTER 22

Gabe was lying on the floor, covered up with the blanket and a pillow under his head just like last time. Only he had bandages around his wrists now. It was dark outside and I cuddled next to Gabe on the floor as I dug deeper into my Uncle's journal. Obviously something good was in here if Bobby wanted it so bad. I just had to figure out where it was. I looked up at the clock and saw it was close to nine. My eyes were getting heavy and I hadn't gotten any closer to finding any useful information. I thumbed through the beginning of the journal and found an entry from before I was born.

May 1991 - Horrible news from Sam today. Our half-brother, Robert, has been causing trouble again. He has become obsessed with Abby over the last couple of months and apparently attacked her in the park yesterday evening on her way home from the library. She is in the hospital after being beaten and raped. How awful. Sam is livid. Hopefully he won't do anything irrational. Robert always was a troubled kid.

"Half-brother?" I spoke out loud. I only knew of Uncle Cooper. I was never aware of another brother. I was wishing Gabe was awake so I had someone to talk to. He was resting peacefully and I didn't want to wake him. I continued reading and, at the same time, trying to keep my eyes open.

June 1991– Abby is pregnant! Sam and her both are filled with joy. I am going to be an Uncle. Abby recovered from her unfortunate meeting with Robert. However, he is nowhere to be found. The cops cannot locate him. He has seemed to disappear. I do fear a little that Sam may have had something to do with his disappearance, but he refuses to talk about anything related to that horrible day.

My eyelids felt like bricks, and I couldn't keep them open any longer. I snuggled closer to Gabe and decided to let sleep enter my mind. However, just as I closed them, I felt a cold drop in temperature around me. My skin had goose bumps suddenly and I opened my eyes to look around the living room. I saw a ghost, crouched down in the corner of the room. It had a blue-aura, and I couldn't see it clearly. I sat up to get a better look. The ghost stood up and headed towards me. I quickly got to my feet and suddenly realized who it was. "Uncle Cooper?" I asked out loud.

"Bekah," he said softly. He gave me a smile and I rushed to meet him.

"Uncle Cooper! I've missed you so much!" I walked right up to him and wanted to hug him so bad. I knew I couldn't, but I still wanted to. I smiled at him and waited for him to speak.

"There are things you don't know about, Bekah. I was hoping you could figure them out by reading my journal, but you don't have time. You're in terrible danger and it grows more dangerous every day. It's time you know what has happened. Give me your hand, Bekah. It's time for a reading," he said to me smiling.

"Why are you sad, Coop?" I asked him. "I thought you left and went to your heaven?"

Cooper looked down at the floor and then back to me. His soft smile remained on his face.

"Bekah, I never left. I knew I had to stay until I was sure you could handle any situation. I love you, Bekah. Now, get in my head," he said.

"No, this couldn't be right." Coop, I saw you. You said good-bye to me and disappeared. I saw you leave," I explained to him.

"Bekah, give me your hand," he said as he held out his. I did as he said, took his hand and started the roller coaster ride in my mind.

I was in my house, only it wasn't my house anymore. It was Cooper's house back before he even knew me. I was on the phone, "What did you do, Sam?" he yelled at the receiver.

"Let it go, Cooper! It's none of your damn business!" Sam yelled back. The line went dead. Cooper slammed the phone down. As he did, memories flooded my brain from his childhood; him and Sam playing happily. Every once in a while a younger kid would come around. He was sad. He never really spoke to either one of them. One day

he was leaving and a man yelled for him, but he took too long to respond. So, the man just came over, grabbed him by the hair and dragged him away. The little boy looked so scared. Cooper didn't know what to do. He was scared for the boy, but he knew better than to try and go against the boy's father.

I fast forward to another time. Cooper was older, probably in his teens. He was handsome. He and Sam continued to hang out like always. They were playing video games when the other boy, now older too, came over once again. He walked into Cooper's room and stood there. He stared at Sam. He wouldn't say a word, just stared at him. Sam finally asked, "What's your problem, dude?" The other boy still wouldn't answer. "Bobby! What the hell, man? What do you want?" Sam yelled at him.

Cooper stepped in between the two teens. "Sam, you don't have to yell. How's it goin, Bobby?" He said as he tossed a glance at him. Again, Bobby just stood there. I focused on Bobby's looks. He was taller than Cooper, had more blond hair and seemed like he was angry. He never smiled or laughed. He looked dirty, like he had worked all day and hadn't cleaned up. He had such a flat effect on his face, like he had no emotion what so ever.

Fast forward again...Cooper was in the hospital with Abby. She looked horrible. Her face was swollen and bruises were forming all over her body. Every time she moved she winced in pain. "Are you sure it was him, Abby?" Cooper asked her.

She responded, "Yes, Cooper, I know what Bobby looks like. It was him." Sam entered the room and I never seen my father look so angry.

"I'll kill him, Coop. I will hunt him down like a dirty rabid dog and kill him." My father spoke very softly, but with much determination and anger in his voice.

Fast forward: Standing in my father's house, Copper asked, "Are you sure the baby's even yours, Sam?" Sam was very clear when he responded to Cooper.

"Don't you even ask that, Coop! Of course it is mine. I wouldn't even have a thought that it belonged to anyone but me!"

Cooper walked towards him and clarified himself, "The timing seems a little odd, don't you think? Or is it better for you not to even think about that, Sam?" Cooper was frustrated and walked out the door of Sam's house. He left him standing in wonder.

Fast Forward: We were at my parent's house again, two years after I had been born. I see myself sitting on the floor. Sam was yelling at Cooper, "You're a freak, Coop. How in the hell can you talk to ghosts? Don't come back around. I don't want you around Bekah," he told him.

Cooper walked towards Sam, "What? I would never hurt Bekah. She's my niece. I want to be a part of her life, Sam!" Cooper was getting angry.

"No! Leave, Cooper. She doesn't see or talk to ghosts. She doesn't even need to know that you exist. GO!" Sam yelled directly at him.

"She's too young to even know if she can do it or not," Cooper tried to reason. He felt so ashamed for his ability to see ghosts. He hadn't asked for it, but he looked one more time at the

small two year old girl playing on the floor, and walked out the door. That was the last time Cooper had seen me until I was seven.

CHAPTER 23

I knew when I jumped out of Cooper's mind I wouldn't be able to talk to him much. So, I talked to him in his head. I sent him waves of good energy and said, "Uncle Cooper, you raised me well. You taught me well. You taught Gabe well, too. I love you so much." I could tell Cooper was sad, but the good energy waves seemed to be helping him.

"Bekah, I have been dealing with this purple ghost for years. It is Bobby. He was our half-brother. Our father had an affair with another woman and she got pregnant. My father wouldn't claim the baby. He was wrong in the way he acted and Bobby grew up very differently than Sam and I did." Cooper took a deep breath in and smiled at Bekah. "I wouldn't ever let anyone harm you, Bekah. I'm so sorry for what happened to your parents, but I'm so grateful I got you back in my life." I continued to add calm, gleeful energy waves into Coopers mind. "Stop it, Bekah. I won't leave until I know this is over. Bobby thinks, just as I suspected, that you are his daughter. He feels that

Sam took you from him. He is very angry and wants revenge," he explained.

"Who killed Bobby, Coop? And if he thinks I'm his daughter, then why does he keep making me undress?" I asked him.

He was a little taken back when he answered, "He is looking for a birthmark on your back. It runs in his family. He's trying to figure out the only way he knows how, if you are his daughter or not," he continued, "I only got a brief look at Bobby's death one time. I know it was horrible and torturous. He clung to life for several days before his murderer let him die. You know who I think it is, Bekah, but I have no proof to credit or discredit the theory. And for the record...you are not his daughter. You look too much like your mother and father to not be theirs. Bobby was obsessed with your mother and you are as beautiful as she was." Cooper looked at me with sympathy. He knew I would be too upset to face the fact that my father had killed Bobby.

"Well, I will deal with that possible fact at a later time. For now, what do I do about Bobby?

He's possessing Gabe constantly. He almost killed him, Cooper. He is very strong, too strong for me. He can put up blocks like I've never seen," I explained to him.

"Yes, he is strong, and he is very sure of himself because I could not stop him. However, you can, Bekah. You and Gabe can do it. You need to go now, Bekah. You've been in here too long. Sleep and let your mind relax," Cooper told me. I could feel him trying to push me out.

"Stop, Coop, I'm not done talking to you. Please, don't. I miss you and I still don't know what to do. Tell me what to do!" I pleaded with him. I could feel myself slipping away. I was exhausted and couldn't stay in his mind much longer.

"You know what to do, Bekah. Finish this. I love you like you were my own daughter. You and Gabe can do it," Cooper said and I went back into my own mind.

I awoke lying on the couch. I had a bit of a headache as I sat up to see what was going on. Gabe rushed to my side. "Bekah, are you okay? You've been sleeping for quite a while." I looked around the living room hoping to see Uncle Cooper and it wasn't all a dream. I was wishing I had all the answers to my questions, but that one, for sure, wasn't true.

I turned my eyes to Gabe and said, "We have so much to talk about. Are you okay, Gabe? Let me see your wrists." I reached for his arms and noticed the bandages were off.

"Yeah, that's the one thing we need to talk about first. What the hell did that damn ghost do to me now? I know it was him, I remember him jumping in," Gabe said. I lightly kissed each of his wrists and got up from the couch.

"Well, next time don't tell me to stop. What the hell were you two talking about anyways?"

Gabe responded, "I'll make the coffee. It sounds like we have a lot to talk about."

It was almost 2pm on Sunday. The sun was shining bright and it was beautiful outside. We sat out on the porch drinking our coffee and discussed everything that happened, from Gabe being possessed to Cooper showing up and talking to me.

We chatted back and forth trying to come up with sensible answers to the questions still left dangling in our minds. The most important question though, "How are we going to defeat him?" spoke across my lips more than once. "I mean, Cooper said we could do it, Gabe, but I still don't know how or what he was talking about." I was frustrated and annoyed. We didn't have a lot of time to work this out. Bobby had already made it very clear he would be back.

Gabe replied, "I'm not sure, Bekah. But I do know that we aren't going to let him get away next time. And he sure as hell won't possess me again. I'm tired of waking up with unknown memories and holes in my body that wasn't there beforehand. That's the last time I will believe him when he says he just wants a few questions answered." I could see the anger in Gabe's face and eyes. I could only imagine what he was going through. "On a happier note," he continued, "I am glad you got to see Cooper. Not real happy he is blue, but he helped out by giving all that information."

Yeah, he helped out...by giving me more questions without answers, I thought to myself.

I walked back into the house and retrieved the journal from under my pillow. There had to be more stuff in here about Bobby. There just had to be. I thumbed through it, looking specifically for entries about him. It felt like a waste of time, but I couldn't just wait around for him to show back up. "We definitely need to stay together, Gabe. No more separating for any reason. We have to watch each other's back. You agree?" I asked while getting comfy on the bed to read.

"Yes, I agree. You read for a bit, and then I will take over to give you a break. Or we can take some other kind of break," he said with a flirtatious grin.

I laughed and replied, "Really? You have two slit wrists and that's what you are thinking about?"

He laughed, grabbed around my waist and pulled me into his chest. "You can't blame a guy for trying." He kissed me and ran his fingers up and down my arms. I could feel the spark of electricity running through my veins and body. It made me feel so much more alive.

"Stop it, Gabe," I laughed and pulled away from him. "Get your head in the right game," I told him. He got off the bed and headed to the front room.

He returned with my laptop. "Fine. I will research on the internet and see if I can come up with anything. It's not as fun, but I will deal with it," he said jokingly.

Two hours later, my head was filled with all kinds of stories from Uncle Cooper and I couldn't take anymore. I tossed the journal at Gabe and said, "Your turn. I will take the laptop." We switched items and Gabe dived right in the journal. "You find anything useful on the 'net?" I asked him.

"Uh, a few myths on how to prevent possession but nothing else," he replied. "You know, the usual salt circle and iron myths. We both know that crap doesn't work," he continued.

It was getting dark outside and both of us were mentally exhausted. I was tired of researching and Gabe was tired of the journal. We both lay back on the bed and took deep relaxing breaths. "We will never figure this out," I said. "Maybe I should just give the book to Bobby and he will leave us alone."

Gabe looked at me with a furrowed brow and said, "No, we aren't doing that, Bekah. He will just continue and you know it. If not torturing us, then he will just torture someone else. We will figure this out." He leaned over and kissed my forehead. A tiny spark flicked on my skin as he did.

"Do you feel that Gabe? Or is it just me?" I asked him not knowing if he even knew what I was talking about.

He stared into my eyes and said, "If you mean the spark, then yes. I feel it. I like it though. Why do you think I am always finding a way to touch you?" He joked back and ran his finger across my cheek and down to my collar bone. I could feel the sparks leave a trail everywhere he touched me. I ran my hand over his chest and to his thigh. He quivered a bit and said, "Yep, I like that!!" and laughed out loud.

I made us dinner and we both sat at the dining room table thinking about the next time we would see Bobby. Neither of us spoke much, as both of us were deep in thought. After we were through, Gabe helped clean up the kitchen and washed the dishes with me.

Immediately after we were done, a breeze of chilly air came over us and we both got goose bumps up our arms. I looked at Gabe and I knew we were both thinking the same thing. I quickly ran over to his side and grabbed his hand. "What are we going to do, Gabe?" I asked with my voice slightly quivering.

"Just stick together, Bekah. We can do this. Even Cooper said we could," He replied with an element of fear and uncertainty in his voice.

"Yeah, just not *how* to do it," I added. "Don't let go of me, Gabe. No matter what, we don't separate."

A purple mist began to assemble in the front room. It swirled like dandy lions in the wind and came to a stop approximately five feet in front of us. The mist came together and formed Bobby, standing tall with a snickering evil smile. He was one ugly guy, I thought to myself. He stood about 6'2", quite a bit taller than Gabe. His hair looked greasy and tangled. He had an unkempt scraggly beard and dirty clothes with rips in them. His eyes were dark brown when he didn't have the flash of purple going through them. I scanned him up and down as soon as he appeared. "Oh, are you not happy to see me? I guess I didn't dress up for our little meeting today. No bother, this won't take long. The journal...now!" he ordered as the mist grew darker and swarmed around his body.

He continued standing in the front room. Gabe and I stood across from him, our hands locked together. "No, Bobby. You can't have the journal. I've been through that thing. Just what the hell do you want it for anyways?" I asked him.

Bobby took a few steps closer to us. "That's none of your damn business, Bekah. This is the last time I will *ask* for it. I will resort to other means, if necessary," he said in an evil, cocky voice. He looked Gabe up and down, "Oh, all the wonderful things I could do to you and you wouldn't even know it until I was done. You can thank that bitch since she won't cooperate." Bobby pointed to me as he moved quickly and ran straight into Gabe. I screamed, "Nooo!"

Bobby hit Gabe and fell back immediately landing on his butt. I quickly glanced at him with a look of shock and wonder. "How did you do that?" I whispered to him.

Gabe whispered back, "I don't know, but put up all your blocks, Bekah, and don't let go of me." I mentally grew a steel wall in my head. I felt odd, not in a bad way, just different.

"Do you feel ok, Gabe?" I asked him. I felt the tingling sparks running up my arm and all over my body. My head was clearer than it had been in weeks. Bobby sat up with a look of shock upon his face.

"You learned your blocks. Well, I'd say it's about time. However, it doesn't matter. All it means is I have to try little harder. No damn problem!" he roared and again ran straight at Gabe.

"Grab him, Bekah!" Gabe yelled at me just as Bobby was close enough to jump into his body. We both raised our free arm, and at the exact same time we grabbed at Bobby's chest.

CHAPTER 24

Gabe and I both went spiraling into a dizzy mind-blowing maze until I felt both of us come to a halt in Bobby's head. "Are you ok, Bekah?" Gabe asked me still trying to get his equilibrium.

"Yeah, I think so. What the hell is happening, Gabe?" I responded back. I was feeling overwhelmed and unsure of myself. This is one thing we hadn't ever done or even planned on doing.

"I don't know, just go with it though. How do we make him leave and never come back?" Gabe yelled.

"I don't know. I have no freaking idea!" I yelled back with feelings of frustration and urgency.

"Well, considering the idea of us jumping in his mind together was never even thought of, I'd say we aren't thinking of other ideas, too," Gabe quickly replied. "There's got to be something,

Bekah! Even your Uncle said we could do it. What are we missing?"

My mind immediately started reading Bobby's. I saw flashes of his life, but in the back of my head I knew exactly what I wanted to find. I scanned everything I could until I came to the memory of my parents. "Bekah, what are you doing? We aren't here to read him. That will take too long. We have to get rid of him!" he said with frustration. I couldn't help it though. My mind knew what it wanted to do, and it was doing it whether I liked it or not.

I was back at the small house I lived in with my parents. I was in my room playing with blocks and toys on the floor. I could see everything. The tattered carpet, messy bed and even the smell of the house entered my senses. It was so weird standing there watching myself as a seven year old little girl. Everything happened with such clarity and insight. I saw myself become tired, and then I felt myself become tired and fell over to the floor. I could feel everything that the younger version of me was feeling.

I was lying there sleeping on the floor when I suddenly saw the purple mist appear just beside me. He stood over me, snickering and planning just before he jumped inside my mind and body. I felt a jolt of danger come across me and then nothing else. I ran to myself across the small bedroom and watched intently. I knew I couldn't do anything, as much as I wanted to. Soon, the little girl stood up, walked into our parent's room and opened the bedside drawer. Her mind was a complete blank, with no thoughts of her own. She had no love in her for anything. She was like a walking dead corpse. I couldn't feel anything, just as the little girl couldn't feel anything of her own.

I was screaming at myself as I watched her pick up the gun. "NO, Bekah! What are you doing?" I kept asking. I tried getting her to stop, but no matter what I did, nothing worked. She continued to walk. I followed her down the hall and into the front room where my parents were enjoying their television show.

I heard Gabe say, "Bekah, you have to stop reading. Stop now, Bekah!" But I couldn't. I knew I should, but I couldn't. Even though I had an ill-conceived notion of what was going to happen, I had to see what occurred next.

As I entered the front room, the little girl version of me held the gun like she knew exactly what she was doing, pointing it at my Dad. She said to him in a very demonic, angry voice, "You brought this upon yourself, Sam. You tortured for days before you killed me!! Now, it's your turn to die!"

My father sat on the couch with a look of pure astonishment and shock on his face. He tossed his half burned cigarette in the ashtray sitting on the coffee table and said, "Bekah, what are you doing, honey? Give Daddy the gun," he pleaded with her. My mother grabbed my father's arm and gave out a small scream.

"What are you doing, Bekah? Please, sweetie, put the gun down. It's very dangerous," my mother added. I could see the fear and confusion on both their faces. The mind of the little seven year old girl was gone. She only had the thoughts of the sick, psychotic Bobby in her head. She had no comprehension of what she was doing or how she was acting. I saw the purple color flash across her beautiful green eyes.

"Abby," said the low, rough voice, "I did nothing but care for you and what did you do in return? You let Sam taint your mind with lies and false tales of me! I only wanted you to love me." I stood, watching and listening to the younger version of me, my hands reaching out trying to grab the gun from the small, delicate younger hands. I knew there was nothing I could do to change the upcoming events, but I felt like I had to try.

"Put that gun down now, young lady!" roared my father, trying to get the attention of his confused daughter.

"Please, Bekah, please, listen to us. Just put the gun down, Sweetie," pleaded my mother as she reached out for her troubled daughter.

"Sit down!" yelled the possessed little girl with a voice not her own. "This is so much more than I dreamed. I really wanted to make you suffer and die a slow death, especially you Sam, but I knew that would be too hard to pull off. But this is working out so much better, having the precious daughter you call yours get my revenge for me!"

My father's face turned from a look of confusion and astonishment to uncertain understanding and anger, "She is NOT your daughter, Bobby! She is mine and always will be!"

"Bobby?" my mother asked. "What the hell is going on, Sam?"

The younger version of me stepped forward, cocked the gun and shot a bullet straight into my father's forehead. He immediately died, falling back on to couch cushion. I screamed at myself and then started screaming at my mother as I knew what was going to happen next. But instead, I watched my mother immediately grab the phone and dial 9–1-1 just before the gun was pointing at her head and the words repeated with such evil vengeance, "All I ever did was love you." The next bullet shot straight through my mother's head. She immediately dropped the phone onto the floor and fell back, remaining in an upright position, next to my father. I once again saw the look on their faces I had nightmares of for so long. The sound of my ear-piercing scream was quickly drowned out by maniacal, evil, satisfying laughter coming from Bobby.

"Bekah!" called Gabe, trying to get my attention. "You have to listen to me!"

I just stood there in front of my parents as the little girl grinned with a sense of accomplishment. She felt no remorse inside her or sorrow for her act. I was powerless to do anything but relive the horrible memory. When she was done marveling at meeting her goal, she left and walked into the kitchen. She removed an old dirty rug and dropped the gun inside some broken floor next to the fridge. She didn't even flinch as the gun thudded on to the gravel crawl space below. She simply returned back to her bedroom. As she stood looking around the room, purple mist started to flow out of her body, separating Bobby. The innocent, unknowingly girl collapsed hard onto the floor.

I was in utter shock and disbelieve, anger and confusion. There are not enough words to explain my feelings of despair. My eyes were burning as the tears couldn't form fast enough to stream down my face. I couldn't stay here any longer. I had to get out. I had an overwhelming feeling of guilt building up inside me. I heard Gabe pleading, "Bekah, it wasn't your fault. Help me get rid of him!"

But I couldn't. I just wanted out of this evil, insane mind. I couldn't wrap my head around things. Everything happened so quickly and my mind was reeling. I could feel the knots forming in my stomach, my head spinning out of control and I knew I what I had to do.

So, I left. I jumped out of his head and back into my own. I heard Gabe yelling, "No, not yet! Just hang on a little longer! It wasn't your fault!!" But it was too late. I had already left and since we were connected by our hands, that meant Gabe left, too. We entered together, kept our bond together, therefore we exited together...

CHAPTER 25

I stood on my own two feet as I entered back into my mind, but I was quickly on the floor. I was screaming, crying and overall angry. My mind continued rapidly spinning and my stomach felt like it was filled with stones. I was dry heaving, sobbing and my entire body was shaking from the evil ghost experience. I saw Gabe sitting next to me trying to regain his composure. "Bekah, please, listen to me," he said with pure desperation in his voice. The room continued to spin as I seen the dark purple mist disappear from the room. I lay back on the floor, drew my knees into my chest and sobbed until I must've fallen asleep.

I awoke in my bed with Gabe's arm around me. Keeping my eyes closed I had thoughts of how wonderful it was having Gabe as my boyfriend and how safe he made me feel when he put him arm around me. I could feel the small sparks everywhere his skin touched mine.

I slowly opened my eyes and looked around the room. All the horrible memories came flooding back. Slowly I removed Gabe's arm and sat on the edge of the bed. My eyes were swollen and my heart ached. The dizziness and nausea was gone, but the guiltiness I felt inside me was beyond bearable. How was I ever going to forgive myself or even wrap the idea of it in my head? I pulled myself up to a standing position when I felt Gabe grab my waist to pull me back down. "No, Gabe! Don't touch me! You saw what I did! How can you even be around me?" I quickly jumped up and ran to the bathroom.

I bent over the sink and turned on the cold water. Tossing as much of it on my face as I could, I wet a washcloth. I could barely see out of my eyes, they were so puffy. Leaning back against the wall I slid to the floor. Holding the cloth over my face, I tried my best to not let any more tears flow. I heard a knock on the door and Gabe opened it. "No, Gabe. Please leave me be!" I yelled at him.

He walked in and sat beside me on the floor. He wrapped his arm around my shoulders and said, "Look, you can yell, you can scream, but I'm right here and I'm not leaving no matter what. So, save your breath, babe." I didn't respond to him. I just sat there with the cloth over my face and felt the sparks of energy across my shoulders.

I have no idea how long we sat on that bathroom floor. My mind continued to run through the memories like a movie reel. The images of my father and mother being shot point blank in the forehead by me seemed more like a nightmare than a reality. I took the cloth off my face and threw it across the bathroom as hard as I could. I really wanted it to smash right through the wall; as if that would make me feel better. I was frustrated and tired of not being able to do anything. As I stood up Gabe asked, "What are you doing, Bekah?"

I glanced down at him, sitting on the floor with a concerned look on his face. I only wanted one thing right now and my mind was focused on getting it. Talking with Gabe was not something I was in the mood for. My anger ranked over every other emotion. I thought it would be better if I said nothing, so I walked away to the living room and stood next to the couch. "Uncle Cooper!" I yelled out. "I know you are still here. Come out and talk to me now!" I yelled at the top of my lungs. I waited, but Uncle Cooper did not show. "Uncle Cooper, I'm not going to stop until you show yourself," I yelled out again. Did he know the truth about what happened to my parents? Did he know I shot them? Did he know I was possessed all those years ago by his crazy, insane half-brother? All these questions roared through my head and I was determined to get the answers.

Gabe said from behind me, "Bekah, he will talk to you when he is ready."

I swung around quickly, "When *he* is ready? Hell with that Gabe! I'm tired of this and I'm really tired of doing things when other people are ready!"

"I'm just saying that maybe if you chill a little bit he would be more apt to come speak with you," Gabe tried to explain.

"You have a house, Gabe, if you don't want to be here, leave." I really didn't care at that moment if I hurt his feelings. Why the hell is he on Uncle Cooper's side anyways? Shouldn't he at least be helping me get answers?

I yelled out again, "Uncle Cooper!" but it was no use. He wasn't showing himself, which only made me assume that the answers to my questions were something I didn't want to hear.

Gabe tried reasoning, "Bekah, I know you are mad, hurt and have lots of questions, but try to take a deep breath and calm down for one moment. You're not thinking rationally," he continued, "Maybe he won't show up because you are so upset."

My anger imploded at him. I quickly replied without much thought, "Gabe, get out of my house! I don't want to see you. I don't want to hear you. I want you to leave!" I turned around with my back towards him. I didn't even want to look at him. I couldn't stand the thought of him even looking at me; eyes filled with pity. I had only one goal at this moment and that was talking to my Uncle.

"Uncle Cooper, I'm still waiting," I said out loud again as I continued to stand in the middle of the room.

"As you wish, Bekah," Gabe stated from behind me and I heard a door slam shut. When I turned around, I noticed my bedroom door was closed. I didn't mean to yell at Gabe, but I really didn't have the patience at this moment to argue. I didn't feel like being rationale or following him to soothe his feelings. What about my feelings? Hell, I just found out I killed my parents! Who was soothing my feelings? Assuming Gabe went in there, I refocused my thoughts on Cooper.

After standing in the living room for over an hour, my back starting to ache and feet beginning to throb, I was starting to lose hope. Uncle Coop obviously wasn't coming around anytime soon and nothing I said was going to make him.

I wandered into the kitchen and started opening cabinets to find something to eat. My shelves were empty, of course, and I sure as heck couldn't ask Gabe for any favors. Not after I just blew up at him. "I'll run out if you want, Bekah," I heard Gabe say behind an open cabinet door. I slammed it shut and seen him standing with his arms crossed over his chest, awaiting an answer.

"I'm not hungry," I replied flatly.

"Then why are you searching through the cabinets? I don't mind going to get some food. I'm pretty hungry myself, too," he continued.

"I said, I'm not hungry, Gabe. Let it be!" I snapped back and leaned up against the kitchen sink.

"Okay, Bekah, you have been screaming at me and yelling for Cooper for the last hour," Gabe continued. "Neither of the two really seems to be working. Cooper isn't showing and you are really pissing me off! I'm trying to remain calm and understanding, but you are seriously making it hard," he replied with a bit of harshness in his tone.

"Yeah, I've realized that," I quietly stated back.

"Really? So you know what you are doing and just don't give a crap?" he asked very seriously.

"Give me a break, Gabe. I'm processing a lot here. I'm not trying to piss you off. I'm trying to get answers to a million questions rummaging through my brain." This wasn't working. I was too far on edge to deal with all these issues at once. I grabbed my car keys and cell phone and headed towards the front door.

"Whoa! Where are you going, Bekah?" Gabe asked.

I grabbed the door knob and slightly turned around, "I don't know, honestly, I have no idea." Turning back around, I felt Gabe grab my arm.

"I sort of thought the whole reason we were with each other, other than *being together*, was to back each other up whenever the psycho ghost comes around. Sorry, you're not going anywhere without me. I may be getting pissed, but not enough to make you defend yourself alone against Bobby," he explained matter-of-factly.

I wandered to the dining room table, put my head down and sulked. Cooper won't come see me and answer any of my questions. I'm hungry and have nothing to eat. Then, on top of it all, my boyfriend is pissed at me. Everything was going to crap! I'm not one to wallow in my own self-pity, but, damn, I did just find out I was used to murder my parents. Don't I get a little bit of leeway?

I felt the keys being removed from my hand. "Let's go, Bekah. Let's go get some food from Del's. You will feel better afterward and your head will be clearer," Gabe suggested. "You can thank me and apologize to me all at once...later," he said with a sweet smile.

I lazily stood up and followed him outside to my SUV. He opened the passenger side door for me and just before I leaned in, I paused and asked him, "What am I apologizing for?"

"You'll think of it later," he chuckled, "after you have food In your belly and realize how crabby you have been," he said with a sweet smile just before getting in and driving off to Del's.

CHAPTER 26

After silently eating chicken fried steaks and mashed potatoes until our aching bellies were full, we made our back home. I, once again, placed my head on the kitchen table and began speaking to Gabe. "You're right. I was quite crabby, if I was to use your words. Bitchy would be more of an appropriate term to use, if you ask me. How'd I end up with someone as great as you? All day I've been yelling and snapping at you, taking my frustrations out on you and still...you are sweet as can be to me."

Gabe responded, "Because I know you. I know when you are frustrated you yell at everything around you and I don't allow myself to take it personal. I can't say I particularly like it," he continued with a brief pause, "but that's what one does when they are in love. I know that eventually you are going to come to your senses and calm down." He had such a nonchalant tone to his voice.

I quickly picked my head up from the table and stared at Gabe. I looked like a mess; my hair was tangled and greasy-feeling. I had dark circles under my eyes from the stress of everything and generally, I felt like a total ass for the way I had been behaving, and here is Gabe, declaring his love for me. I couldn't stop staring at him, "Why? How can you even say that? I'm a train wreck, Gabe!" I blurted out as my eyes filled with tears.

"Bekah, you may feel like lower than dirt now, but who wouldn't after everything you have been through? It doesn't define you; it just makes you stronger and wiser. I am lucky to have you," he said with such compassion. I stood up from the table and allowed myself to enjoy his gentle embrace. His hugged warmed my heart and for just a moment I let my mind forget all the bad things that had happened.

"I love you, too, Gabe," I replied with sincere honesty. He cupped my face with his warm, gentle hands. Sweet and softly he kissed me and I knew I was the luckiest girl in the world.

As I parted from Gabe to make my way into the front room, I saw Uncle Cooper standing in the corner. "You always were quite persistent, Bekah. I'm sorry I didn't come sooner. I felt you needed time to calm yourself. I'm right here. Though, I have no idea what I could possibly do or say to relieve your anger and sorrow." Slightly raising one eyebrow as he glanced at the both of us and allowing a small grin to form, he asked, "However, you are obviously in the middle of something and I didn't mean to intrude. Shall I return at a better time?" His eyes darted to Gabe and he seemed to have a sense of satisfaction come over his face.

I took a deep, cleansing breath and walked up to him. "No, you can stay and if you want to help, you can start by answering a few questions, Uncle Coop. Did you know the truth about what happened to my parents?" I continued. "That I was possessed by Bobby and I pulled the trigger that killed them so many years ago?" I asked with a low, calm voice.

I knew the answer by the look of shock on Uncle Cooper's face. "No, Bekah, I did not know that. I'm so sorry, but if he possessed you, then in no way was the shooting your fault. You must believe that, right? Sometimes seeking out the truth doesn't lead to what we want it to."

"I don't know what to believe right now, Uncle Coop. This has all happened so fast. I just want it all to stop and give me time to catch up. However, I can't allow that right now. Gabe and I beat Bobby at his own game. We did it together, just like you said." I took a deep breath in and continued, "But it isn't over. Next question: how do you suppose I could send Bobby to hell?" I asked with a low, vengeful tone.

"Bekah, what makes you think you can send a ghost to hell? You help bring peace to restless ghosts and send them on to their heaven, but never have I, or anyone I know of, sent a ghost straight to hell. I don't know if that is even possible," Cooper responded with concern as he continued to stand in the corner of the room with his blue aura swirling around him. "Hello, Gabe, it's good to see you."

"If the veil to heaven is thin here, then it would only stand to reason that the veil to Hell is just the same. Does that not seem feasible to you?" I explained.

"Hey, Coop, how's it going? I'll leave you two be so you can chat," Gabe answered back just before entering the bedroom and shutting the door.

I continued as if I wasn't interrupted, "If I can push a ghost to their heaven, then I should be able to push a ghost to Hell. Seems reasonable to me," I continued. "Together, Gabe and I can do things that one Ghost Reader cannot. I will send Bobby to Hell, Uncle Coop, with or without your help." Feeling a little hopeless I sat on the couch. "You cannot possibly imagine how I am feeling right now. To know what I did, possessed or not, it's killing me inside. Bobby must pay for his actions. I will deal with mine at a later date," I stated to Cooper.

Cooper moved closer and sat next to me on the couch. "Revenge is a strong emotion and you cannot let it steer your intentions, Bekah. It is not up to you to punish Bobby or judge anyone. You and Gabe have an unheard power, but because of that you both must be very careful. This power hasn't been shown before. It is unknown what else you two are capable of doing."

I listened to his words, but they didn't set well in my head. Why can't I punish him? After all, he took it upon himself to intertwine his life with mine. He decided all those years ago to take revenge into his own hands and used me to execute that revenge. I could not at this time agree with my Uncle. "Well, I guess it is time to find out, isn't it, Uncle Coop?" I asked him, as I set my mind to doing the unheard of.

CHAPTER 27

"Gabe!" I hollered. No response from him. Maybe he was still mad at me. I was most certainly hateful to him and I felt horrible for it; yet another thing to add to my list of things to forgive myself for. "Seriously, Gabe, we need to get to work." I walked to my bedroom door and opened it. After looking around the room I realized Gabe wasn't there. The window was closed and nothing seemed out of place. "Where are you?" I asked with curiosity. Immediately I went to the closed bathroom door. Jerking it open, I saw Gabe standing by the sink looking very unhappy, and Bobby with his thick, purple-black aura swirling around him.

"Hello, Bekah. I thought we needed to talk and there's no better way to get your attention than using your little boy-toy...so, let's chat," Bobby said with a sneer. Gabe swung his fist into the air, throwing the most powerful right hook he could, but Bobby immediately jumped into Gabe's body. Gabe's ocean blue eyes flashed a deep purple color and stared directly at me.

I couldn't show any weakness or fear because after all that is what Bobby thrived upon.

Before he got any words out I stated, "Really? You're back to that little trick? You know damn well I can yank you out. So, I'm thinking no to the chat and as I said before, it's time to get to work," raising my voice to a yell, "Time for your reign of terror to end!"

I quickly stepped forward to Gabe, whom just as swiftly stepped back. "You never learn Bekah, do you? You may want to watch yourself. I can and will hurt Gabe as you well know. So let's be civil and talk for a moment." Just as he stopped talking he grabbed his left middle finger with his right hand and snapped it sideways. "Oh, that actually kind of feels good," Bobby said with a cynical chuckle.

I shut my eyes, turned my head away and wished I never seen the man I loved getting hurt. After I briefly jumped at the sound of the cracking bone, I replied, "What do you want, Bobby?" I was seriously getting tired of playing this game. Things had to come to an end with Bobby's rampage.

"I want to make it very clear what I can do if you even try to send me to Hell," he continued. "Oh, yes, Bekah, I heard your conversation with dear old Uncle Cooper. He's right, you know? You can't just simply send me to Hell because you wish it. You don't have that kind of power." He grabbed the next finger and snapped it just like the first as he casually paced on the bathroom floor.

"Is there no such thing as a private conversation in this place anymore?" I quickly smarted.

"I'm pretty sure Gabe will be feeling that pain soon," Bobby said plainly, "and no, there isn't, Bekah. Not when I am the main topic."

Again, I winced at the snapping sound of Gabe's bones cracking apart. I felt myself becoming desperate and started thinking that this would never end. Every day Bobby could show up and hurt Gabe however he wanted, or anyone for that matter. Bobby could manipulate me for the rest of my life. I would have to continue to see the man I love suffer through pain and agony all because Bobby is able and happy to do it. This had to end right here and now before Gabe received any more broken bones or body parts. As Bobby turned to pace his way across the bathroom floor I knew this was probably my only chance. I leapt forward, ensuring I grabbed Gabe's good hand. I instantly felt the tingling sensation shoot up my arm. I knew I made the connection with him I needed. Opening my mind, I spiraled into the roller coaster maze and stopped abruptly in Bobby's evil, sinister head.

"Ah, this is a better place for a chit-chat, don't you think, Bobby?" I said, and then not knowing exactly what I was even doing, I immediately started shoving thoughts and images into Bobby's mind to cross over the veil that was hopefully just below him.

I could feel Bobby fighting me, his anger intensifying and his voice echoing through my mind, "No! You cannot do that. You are not strong enough and don't have that kind of control! You are only a Ghost Reader, Bekah. Not a Sender of Souls like Ellie was," Bobby roared at me.

I ignored my stomach curling in nausea and the throbbing pain in my head as I concentrated to push Bobby further down. Ellie? Who is Ellie I briefly thought, but quickly I went back to concentrating on Bobby.

I looked below at Bobby's feet and seen a black spider web-like flooring. It had arms stretching out of it, trying to reach through the veil. Instantly I knew that was the veil I had to shove him through. With every notion and thought in my head, I became angrier. I did want revenge for what he had done to my parents, to Gabe and to me. I could feel the fury inside me boiling. "NO!" Bobby thundered at me. I saw him inch away from the veil I was working so hard to move him towards. He was definitely stronger than me. I started to doubt myself on whether or not I could really do this. However, at that exact moment, I started to feel stronger. My mind felt electric shocks flitter through it and I knew I was no longer alone in this fight.

"You're right, Bobby. She's just a Ghost Reader who doesn't have the power to banish you…alone, but she isn't alone now, is she?" Gabe sneered with confidence. I felt Bobby move, his body being forced down towards the web-like veil. Both Gabe and I had our minds locked on Bobby's, pushing him closer and closer.

"You are a foolish, arrogant excuse of a man. Even with you at her side, it will not be enough!" Bobby bellowed with conviction to Gabe. However, Bobby didn't move away from the veil, but instead consistently down towards it. I could see the look of shock come over his face and he instantly yelled with all his might, "NO!" When he did this, he moved up a few inches and unleashed a disturbing laugh.

I didn't start to worry at this point as Bobby would have to keep very strong to continue this fight and he was starting to wear down. Through the evil sneer on his face and maniacal laugh, he had a hint of worry in his eyes; a furrowed brow as shock and disbelieve took over his thoughts. I knew he wasn't going to win and I could tell he was starting to believe it too.

Of course, I may have gotten too cocky because what happened next totally through my whole train of thought. Bobby got angry...really angry. His aura bubbled, steamed and spit redness as he flung himself up towards both Gabe and I. "I'm not going alone, Bitch," he roared at me as he grasped my ankle and took off towards the spider webbed veil. I felt a pull as my hand separated from Gabe's hold.

"Bekah!" Gabe frantically shouted. Both Gabe and I saw the mind of Bobby's becoming hazy. We couldn't stay in here unless we were bond by each other. We gave each other strength and now that we were separated, we were both becoming weak.

I was the frantic one now. I saw the webbing coming closer and closer. I had no idea what to do. My mind was reeling with unfinished thoughts and ideas of how to get out of this mess. I saw Gabe attempting to catch up with us, reaching out to me and trying to grab any part of me he could. He was so close to grabbing my hand, but no matter how much I stretched and reached out to him, I couldn't make up those few inches between us.

I felt Bobby hit the veil first. It slowed both of us just enough for Gabe to make contact with my arm. He grasped it tightly and we both felt our minds connect, instantly becoming stronger. I looked down at Bobby and I saw the black arms reaching up and grabbing his leg, pulling him down farther. As Bobby was distracted, Gabe pulled as hard as he could and I broke loose from his grasp.

As he held me close, safely wrapped in his arms, Bobby fought the reaching arms, kicking his legs and yelling, "No!" over and over. We could see Bobby's legs being slowly swallowed by black spider webbing. It crawled up his leg devouring every inch of him as it worked towards pulling him through the veil.

In all the excitement, though, both Gabe and I wasn't focusing on pushing Bobby down and Bobby was definitely fighting to get back up. He made progress, too, and by the time we realized it, Bobby was head to head even with us again. Laughing loudly and manically, he held up one particular finger, showing us exactly what he thought.

I pulled Gabe's face down to me to get his attention. "We have to get it together, Gabe...focus!" I yelled and we both started shoving the thoughts of crossing over the wicked veil below back into Bobby's head. He started falling again, closer and closer to the veil. This time Gabe and I knew to keep our distance from him.

We were doing it. He was so close that the arms were reaching out again, making loud, and screeching noises as they tried to find their latest victim. We could taste victory in our minds and I couldn't help but smile a little bit.

Suddenly a blur of blue aura surrounded us and it streaked in a downward spiral. I heard Uncle Cooper's voice fill my mind, "I will take it from here, Bekah. Know that I have always loved you like you were my own daughter. He cannot be allowed to roam amongst the living anymore." Uncle Cooper reached his arms out and surrounded Bobby in his aura. With a flash of light Uncle Cooper tore through the veil and Bobby, along with Cooper, fell into the darkness below as they were both being tangled and wrapped in the dark webbing.

"NO! Uncle Coop, what are you doing? We had this! Come back!" I screamed as loud as I could.

I rushed to just above the webbed veil as Gabe pulled me back stating, "No, Bekah, you can't get any closer." As we noticed the arms starting to stretch outward again, grasping anything it could find, I heard a faint evil laugh that I was sure belonged to Bobby, as they both disappeared and the webbed veil magically sewn itself back together.

ABOUT THE AUTHOR

Anne Dehn currently resides and works as a nurse in Harrisonville, MO. Her recent and new found passion for writing resulted in this book. She has three wonderful children and has been married to her high school sweetheart for 18 years. If you have any comments or questions regarding this book please email:

Ghostreader76@yahoo.com

Anne enjoys hearing any feedback or constructive criticism. Hope you enjoyed this story and keep your eye out for the second book in the series coming soon.